THE DEVIL'S GRIN

Anna Kronberg Book 2

ANNELIE WENDEBERG

Cover: Nuno Moreira

Editing: Tom Welch

ISBN-13: **978-1481262262**

Bonus material at the end of this book:
Preview of **_The Fall_** - Anna Kronberg Book 3

The World of Anna Kronberg

Step into my time machine and join Anna on her hunt for the killer!

www.silent-witnesses.com

All the silent witnesses ... the place, the body, the prints ... can speak if one knows how to properly interrogate them.

Alexandre Lacassagne

The Devil's Grin was awarded the *Blue Carbuncle* by the German Sherlock Holmes Society for best Sherlock Holmes Mystery 2014.

Thanks, you crazy bunch of Holmes fans!!!

Foreword

I never considered writing anything but science papers — not until my family and I moved into a house with a history dating back to 1529. While ripping off modern improvements to restore some of the building's historic charm, we found a treasure. Hidden underneath the attic's floorboards, resting in thick layers of clay, sand, and larch needles, were a dozen slender books bound in dark leather. These turned out to be the journals of an extraordinary woman.

Reading her story left me shocked, awed, and wishing I might ever be as courageous as she. I've respected her wish to not reveal her identity. Instead, I've mixed the names of a friend, a German beer (sorry about that), and the last part of my family name to end up with 'Anna Kronberg.'

People close to Anna, such as her father and her lover, bear false names as well, while others, better known, keep their true identities.

History is indeed little more than the register of the crimes, follies, and misfortunes of mankind.
    E. Gibbon

I have finally found the peace to write down what must be revealed. At the age of twenty-seven, I witnessed crimes so heinous that no one dared tell the public. It has never been put down in ink on paper — not by the police, newspapermen, or historians. The general reflex was to forget what happened.

I will hide these journals in my old school, hoping that they'll be found one day and made public. These crimes must be revealed and future generation warned. And I wish as well to paint a different picture of the man who came to be known as the world's greatest detective.

Summer 1889

One of the first things I learned as an adult was that knowledge and fact mean nothing to people who have been subjected to an adequate dose of fear and prejudice.

This simple-mindedness is the most disturbing attribute of my fellow two-legged creatures. According to Alfred Russel Wallace's newest theories, I belong to this same species — the only one among the great apes that has achieved bipedalism and developed an unusually large brain. As there is no other upright, big-headed ape, I must be human. Though I have my doubts.

My place of work — the ward for infectious diseases at Guy's Hospital in London — is a prime example of the aforementioned human bias against facts. Visitors would show their delight as they entered through the elegant wrought-iron gate. Once on the hospital grounds, they were favourably impressed by a generous court with lawn, flowers, and bushes. The white-framed windows spanned floor to ceiling, showing bright and well-ventilated wards that gave the illusion of a pleasant haven for the sick.

Yet, even the untrained eye should not have failed to notice a dense overpopulation: each of the forty cots in my ward was occupied by two or three patients, bonded together by their bodily fluids, oozing either from infected wounds or raw orifices. Due to chronic limitations of space, doctors and nurses disregarded what they knew about disease transmission under crowded conditions, and death spread like fire in a dry pine forest.

The staff considered the situation acceptable simply through habit. Any change would have required an investment of energy and consideration, neither willingly spent for anyone but oneself.

Therefore, nothing ever changed.

If I'd had a yet more irascible temperament than the one I already possessed, I would have openly held hospital staff responsible for the deaths of countless patients who succumbed from lack of proper care and hygiene. But then, those who entrusted us with their health and well-being might share a portion of the guilt, as it was common knowledge that the mortality of patients in hospitals was at least twice that of those who remained at home.

Sometimes I wondered how these people could possibly have got the idea that medical doctors were able to help. Although circumstance occasionally permitted me to cure disease, this sunny Saturday seemed to hold no such prospect.

The wire a nurse handed me complicated matters further: *To Dr Kronberg: Your assistance is required. Possible cholera case at Hampton Waterworks. Come at once. Inspector Gibson, Scotland Yard.*

I WAS A BACTERIOLOGIST AND EPIDEMIOLOGIST, one of the best to be found in England, a fact due mostly to a paucity of scientists working in this very young field of research. In all of London, we were but three, the other being my former students. For the occasional cholera fatality or for any other victim who seemed to have been felled by an angry army of germs, I was invariably summoned.

As these calls came with some frequency, I had the occasional pleasure of working with the Metropolitan Police. They were a well-mixed bunch of men whose mental sharpness ranged from that of a butter knife to an overripe plum.

Inspector Gibson belonged to the plum category. The butter knives, fifteen in total, had been assigned to the murder division — a restructuring effort within the Yard in response to the recent Whitechapel murders and the hunt for the culprit commonly known as Jack the Ripper.

I slipped the wire into my pocket and asked the nurse to summon a hansom. Then I made my way down to my basement laboratory and the hole in the wall that I called my office. I threw a few belongings into my doctor's bag and rushed to the waiting cab.

THE DRIVER INSISTED on hitting every single pothole on the way to Hampton Water Treatment Works, yet I did enjoy the ride, for it offered contentments long lost in London: greenery, fresh air, and once in a while, a glimpse of a river reflecting sunlight. As soon the Thames entered London, it turned into the dirtiest stretch of moving water in all of England. As it crawled through the city, it became saturated with cadavers of all of the many species that populated the city, plus their excrements. The river washed them out to the sea, where they sank into the deep to be forgotten. London's endless supply of filth seemed enough to defile the Thames for centuries to come. At times, this tired me so much that I felt the urge to pack my few belongings and move to a remote village. Perhaps to start a practice or breed sheep — or do both — and be happy. Unfortunately, I was a scientist and my brain needed exercise. Country life would soon become dull, I was certain.

The hansom came to a halt at a wrought-iron gate with a prominent forged iron sign arching above it, its two sides connecting to pillars of stone. Behind it stretched a massive brick complex adorned by three tall towers. I alighted and stepped onto a dirt road. Roughly half a mile east of me, a reservoir was framed by crooked willows and a variety of tall grasses. My somewhat elevated position allowed me to look upon the water's dark blue surface that was decorated with hundreds of white splotches. The whooping, shrieking, and bustling about identified them as water birds. A low humming seeped through the open doors of the pumping station. Apparently, water was still being transported to London. A rather unsettling thought, considering the risk of cholera transmission.

Hampton Water Treatment Works was a prime example of the inertness of the government whenever money was to be invested or consideration given. It had taken Thomas Telford — a progressive and brilliant engineer — more than two decades to convince the authorities that Londoners had been drinking their own filth for much too long, that taking Thames water resulted in recurring cholera outbreaks and other gruesome diseases, and that a sufficient supply of clean drinking water was urgently needed.

Three police officers stood on the walkway to the main building — two blue-uniformed constables and one in plain clothes, he being Gibson. The bobbies answered my courteous nod with nods of their own, while Gibson pulled his mouth to a shape that looked like a drunken comma, held up a hand, and watched me walk past him.

I aimed for a man who, I hoped, was a waterworks employee. He was a bulky yet healthy looking specimen, perhaps sixty or seventy years of age. A face framed by bushy white whiskers and mutton chops was topped up with eyebrows of equal consistency. He gave the impression of someone who would retire only when already dead. And he was looking strained, as though his shoulders bore a heavy weight.

'Good day to you. My name is Dr Anton Kronberg. The police summoned me to examine a potential cholera fatality. I assume you are the chief engineer?'

'Yes, sir. William Hathorne's the name. Pleased to make

your acquaintance.' We shook hands, and then he added, 'It was me who found the dead man.'

Behind me, Gibson made an indignant noise and began talking to his constables. I guessed he felt I had undermined his authority yet again. Unsurprising, for it would likely have required a greater degree of learning ability on his part to have become accustomed to my impertinence.

'Was it you who claimed the man to be a cholera victim?' I enquired.

'Yes. It was very...obvious.'

'But the pumps are still running.'

'Open cycle. Nothing is being transported to London at the moment,' Mr Hathorne supplied.

'May I ask what makes you think he had cholera?'

He coughed, dropped his gaze to the grass by his shoes. 'I lived on Broad Street.'

We stared at the vegetation for a moment, and I wondered whether the loss of a wife or child had burned the haggard and bluish look of cholera death into his memory. A few years before I was born, the water from a public pump on Broad Street had killed more than six hundred people, marking the end of London's last cholera epidemic. A cesspit had been dug too close to the public pump, allowing the disease to spread quickly. As soon as both pump and cesspit were shut down, the epidemic ceased.

'I am sorry,' I said softly. With a tightening chest, I wondered how many people would die if massive amounts of cholera germs should ever spread through London's drinking water supply. But these waterworks were far away from the city, and the great mass of water over distance would dilute the germs to an undetectable and harmless level before ever reaching London. As very few people dared drink directly from the river, an epidemic was unlikely.

I straightened up. 'Did you move the body, Mr Hathorne?'

'Well, I had to. I couldn't let him float in that trench, could I?'

'You used your hands, I presume.'

'What else would I use? My teeth?' Naturally, Mr Hathorne looked puzzled.

While explaining that I must disinfect his hands, I bent down and extracted the bottle of creosote and a large handkerchief from my bag. A little stunned, he let me proceed.

'You strike me as a man who keeps his eyes and ears open. Would you be able you tell me who else touched the man? It's important to know, to prevent the disease from spreading.'

With shoulders squared and moustache bristling, he replied, 'All the police officers, and that other man over there.' His furry chin jerked towards the ditch.

I turned around and spotted the man Hathorne had indicated. He was tall and unusually lean, and for a brief moment I almost expected him to be bent by the wind and sway back and forth in synchrony with the high grass surrounding him. He was making his way up to the river and soon disappeared into thick vegetation.

Gibson approached, hands in his trouser pockets, face balled to a fist. 'Dr Kronberg.'

'Just a moment,' I said and turned back to the engineer.

'Mr Hathorne, am I correct in assuming that the pumps — when not running in open cycle — take water from the reservoir and not directly from the trench?'

'Yes, that is correct.'

'So the contaminated trench water that had already entered the reservoir, should have been greatly diluted?'

'Of course. But...who knows how long the dead fella was floating in there.'

'Is it possible to reverse the direction of the water flow and flush the trench water back into the Thames?'

He considered my question, pulled his whiskers, then nodded.

'Can you exchange the entire trench volume three times?'

'I certainly can. But it would take the whole day...' He looked as though he hoped I would change my mind.

'Then it will take the whole day,' I said. 'Thank you for your help, Mr Hathorne.' We shook hands, then I turned to Gibson. 'Inspector, I will examine the body now. If you would show me the way?'

Gibson squinted at me, tipped his head a fraction, then lead the way up the path.

'I will take a quick look at the man. If he is indeed a cholera victim, I will need you to get me every man who touched his body.' After a moment of consideration, I added, 'Forget what I said. I want to disinfect the hands of every single man who has been in the waterworks today.'

Gibson didn't like to talk too much in my presence. We had cultivated a mutual dislike. Backed up by his underlings, he pretended to be hard-working, intelligent, and dependable — but was none of that. He must have won his position as a police inspector as the son of someone important, because only few men were as unqualified as he.

We followed a narrow path alongside the broad trench that connected the river to the reservoir. I wondered about its purpose — why store water when great quantities of it flowed past every day? Perhaps because moving water was turbid and the reservoir allowed the dirt to settle and the water to clear? I would ask Hathorne about it.

Gibson and I walked through grass that was tall enough that should I stray off the path (and I felt compelled to do so) its tips would tickle my chin. Large dragonflies whizzed past me, one almost colliding with my forehead. They did not seem to be accustomed to human invasion. The chaotic concert of water birds carried over from the nearby reservoir.

A nervous screeching of small sandpipers mingled with the trumpeting of swans and the melancholic cries of a brace of cranes, and brought back very old memories.

These pretty thoughts were wiped away instantly by a whiff of sickly-sweet decomposition. The flies had noticed it, too, and a cloud of them accompanied us as we approached a discarded-looking pile of clothes framing a man's bluish face. Fish had carved him an expression of utter surprise. Lips, nose, and eyelids were gnawed off. He must have spent a considerable time floating face down.

The wind turned a little, and the stink hit us directly. Gibson pressed a handkerchief to his mouth and nose.

'Three policemen are present. Why so many?' I asked him. 'And who is the tall man who darted off to the Thames? Is this a case of suspected murder?'

The inspector dropped his chin to reply as someone behind me cut across in a polite yet slightly bored tone, 'A dead man could not have climbed a fence.'

Surprised, I turned around and had to crane my neck. The man who had spoken was a head taller than I and wore a sharp and determined expression. He continued in the same bored, but slightly amused tone, 'And so Inspector Gibson concluded that someone must have shoved the body into the waterworks. He further concluded that this was done to cause a panic. Everyone remembers the Broad Street epidemic. Gibson summoned as many men as he possibly could on such short notice to assist him, and to keep this from the press. As we all know from experience, the number of people involved in a secret is directly proportional to the distance said secret will travel.' His mouth twitched.

Keen, light grey eyes pierced mine for a moment, and then slid away. Apparently, nothing of interest had presented itself. I was greatly relieved. At that moment, I couldn't help but fear that he might see through my disguise. But, as usual, I was surrounded by blindness.

The sharp contrast between the two men in front of me was almost ridiculous. Gibson seemed to lack facial muscles and his lower lip was more rain gutter than communication tool. He almost constantly worked his jaws, picked and chewed his nails, and perspired on the very top of his skull.

The other man, highly alert, seemed to consider himself a superior specimen, judging from the way he talked about Gibson in his presence (although, I had to confess, I would likely have done the same), and by the self-confidence he exuded that bordered on arrogance. His attire and demeanour bespoke a man who had enjoyed a spoiled upper class upbringing.

Gibson lowered the handkerchief and wiped the frown off his face. 'Mr Holmes, this is Dr Anton Kronberg, epidemiologist from Guy's.'

I held out my hand, which was taken, squeezed firmly, and quickly dropped as though infected. 'Dr Kronberg, this is Mr Sherlock Holmes,' finished the inspector, making it sound as though I should know who Sherlock Holmes was.

I gave the man a nod, and asked if the body had indeed been pushed into the trench.

'Unlikely,' Mr Holmes answered.

'How can you be sure?'

'There are no marks on either side of the Thames water's edge, the body shows no signs of being transported with a hook, rope, a boat, or similar, and...' He trailed off, and I made a mental note to go and check the Thames's flow to ascertain that a body could indeed have floated into the trench without help.

Mr Holmes narrowed his eyes at me. His gaze flew from my slender hands to my small feet, swept over my slim figure and my not-very-masculine face. Then his attention got stuck on my flat chest for a second. A last look at my throat, the nonexistent Adam's apple hidden behind a high collar and cravat, and his eyes flared with surprise. A slight smile flickered across his face while his head produced an almost imperceptible nod.

Suddenly, my clothes felt too small, my hands too clammy, my neck too tense, and the rest of my body too hot. I was itching all over, and had to force myself to keep breathing. Had he just discovered my secret? In these few minutes? It couldn't be, could it? I'd fooled everyone else for years. No one had ever guessed who I was. Or *what* I was, I should say.

I took a deep breath. I was surrounded by policemen, and if I had indeed been discovered, my fate was sealed. I would lose my occupation, my degree, and my residency to spend a few years in jail. When finally released, I would do what? Embroider doilies?

Before doing something reckless and stupid, I pushed past the two men and made for the Thames. I would have to deal with Holmes when he was alone. The notion of knocking him on his head and throwing him into the river appeared very attractive, but I flicked the silly thought away and forced myself to focus on the business at hand.

First I needed to know how the body could possibly have got into that trench. The grass was intact. No blades were bent except for where I had seen Mr Holmes walking along. I looked around on the ground, somewhat irritated that Mr Holmes was observing my movements. Only one set of footprints was visible, which must belong to Mr Holmes. I picked up a few rotten branches and dry twigs, broke them into pieces of roughly arm's length, and cast them into the Thames. Most of them made it into the trench and drifted towards me. A sand bank was producing vortices just at the mouth of the trench, causing my floats to enter the trench instead of being carried away by the much greater force of the river. Chances were good that it was only the water that had pushed the body in.

'Your assertion might be correct, Mr Holmes,' I noted while passing him. He didn't appear bored anymore. That could only mean he was making plans on whether to black-mail me or report me to the police straight away.

As I walked back to the corpse, my stomach felt as if I had eaten a brick.

The exposed skin of the dead man indicated that he'd been in the water for approximately thirty-six hours. I knelt and opened my bag. Mr Holmes squatted down on the oppo-site side, too close to the body for my taste.

'Don't touch it,' I said.

He showed no reaction, just swept his gaze over the dead man.

To better gauge Mr Holmes's character and my chances of remaining undiscovered, or perhaps simply because I was nervous, I made conversation. 'Do you happen to know how fast the Thames flows here, Mr Holmes?'

Without looking up he muttered, 'Thirty miles from here at the most.'

'Considering which duration of exposure?'

'Twenty-four to thirty-six hours.'

'Interesting. Do you have a medical education?' He had correctly assessed the time the man had spent in the water. He had also calculated the maximum distance the corpse could have travelled downstream.

'Merely that of a layman.' He crouched lower, screwing his eyes half-shut.

I got the impression that he vibrated with an intellectual energy wanting to be utilised. 'Are you an odd version of a private detective? You must be. The police never call them in. At least, I've never heard of them doing so.'

'I prefer the term *consulting detective*.' He looked up briefly, somewhat absent-mindedly, then turned his attention back to the corpse.

'I see.' I, too, turned my attention back to the body. The man was extremely emaciated. His skin had the typical blue tinge and looked paper-thin. This was most definitely cholera in the final stage. I reached out, about to examine his clothes for signs of violence when Mr Holmes barked a sharp, 'Wait!'

Before I could protest, he yanked a magnifying glass from his waistcoat pocket, elbowed me aside, and hovered over the corpse. The fact that his nose almost touched the man's coat was rather unsettling. 'He must have been dressed by someone else,' he said.

'Was he now.'

Looking a little irritated, he held out his magnifying glass to me, an eyebrow at a mocking angle. I wiped my hands on the grass and took the offered tool.

Mr Holmes started to talk rather fast then. 'The man was obviously right-handed — that hand having more calluses on the palms, and appearing generally stronger. Yet you will observe greasy thumbprints pushing in from the left-hand side of his coat buttons.'

I spotted the prints, put my nose as close as possible, and sniffed — corpse smell, Thames water, and possibly the faintest hint of petroleum hiding underneath the aforementioned stink. 'Petroleum. Perhaps from an oil lamp,' I muttered more to myself.

Examining his hands, I found superficial scratches, swelling and bruises on the knuckles of the right hand. Probably from a fist fight only a day or two before his death — odd, given his weakness. His hands seemed to have been strong and rough once, but had not been doing hard work for a while now, for the calluses had started to peel off. His fingernails had multiple discolourations, showing that he had been undernourished and sick for weeks before contracting cholera. He must have been living in extreme poverty before he died. I wondered where he had come from. His clothes were tattered and a size too large. Debris from the river had collected in folds and pockets. I examined his sleeves, turned his hands around, and found a pale red banding pattern around his wrists.

'Restraint marks,' said Mr Holmes. 'This man used to be a farm worker, but lost his occupation three to four months ago.'

'Maybe,' I said. He must have based his judgement on the man's clothes, boots, and hands. 'However, the man could have had any other physically demanding occupation. He could as well have been a coal miner. The clothes are not necessarily his.'

Mr Holmes sat up. 'We can safely assume that he owned these boots for about a decade.' He pulled off a boot and held it next to a pale and wrinkled foot. The sole, worn down to a thin layer of rubber, contained a major hole where the man's heel used to sit, and showed a perfect imprint of the shape of the man's foot and toes. The shape of a thick callus on the man's heel fit perfectly the hole in the sole.

'I figured that you must have taken a close look at him before I arrived, for you spoke about the lack of signs of transport by a boat, a hook, or rope. Now it appears you've touched and even undressed the corpse?'

'It was but a superficial examination. I found it more pressing to investigate how the body entered the trench.'

I blew out a breath. 'You have put your hands to your face at least twice, even scratched your chin very close to your lips. Quite reckless, don't you think? It is rather likely that his clothes are contaminated with faecal germs — an unfortunate circumstance of uncontrollable diarrhoea.'

His gaze darted to the corpse, then to his hands, and to my face. I passed him a handkerchief soaked in creosote and he wiped himself off with care. Then, without further comment on the matter, he bent low over the corpse yet again, and pointed at something. 'What is this?'

I picked at the smudge he had indicated. It was a small green feather that was tucked into a small tear just below the coat's topmost buttonhole. I smoothed it and rubbed off the muck.

'From an oriole female. How unusual! I haven't heard their call for many years.'

'A rare bird?' he asked.

'Yes, but I can't tell where this feather has have come from. I have never heard this bird's call in the London area. The man could have found the feather far away from here, could have been carrying it around for quite a while...' I trailed off, examining the small quill and the light grey down.

'The quill is still somewhat soft,' I murmured, 'and the down is not worn. This feather wasn't plucked by a bird of prey or a fox or the like; it was moulted. He had it for a few weeks at most, which means he must have found it just before he became ill, or someone gave it to him while he was sick.'

Surprised, Mr Holmes sat back, and I felt an odd urge to explain myself. 'In my childhood I spent rather too much time in treetops, and learned a lot about birds. The quill tip shows that the feather has been pushed out by a newly emerging one. Most songbirds begin moulting in late spring. The farther north they live, the later moulting starts. The bird must have shed this feather in late spring or midsummer this year. Wherever this man spent his last days is close to the nesting place of an oriole pair. A female is never alone at that time of year.'

'Where do these birds live?' he enquired.

'In old forests, where water is nearby, such as a lake or a stream. An adjacent wetland would do, too.'

'The Thames?'

'Possibly,' I mused, and was suddenly reminded of the lurking danger. The brick in my stomach became unbearable. I didn't know if he had truly seen what was behind my facade, but I had to know. 'Are you planning to give me away?'

There was not a trace of surprise or puzzlement. Instead, he looked amused. He knew precisely what I meant. 'You don't fancy going to India, I presume.' It wasn't so much a question as a statement. The few British women who had managed to get a medical degree, eventually gave in to the mounting social pressure and left for India, out of the way of the exclusively male medical establishment.

'No, I do not. You have not answered my question.'

'If I believed in the validity of all our societal norms and fashions, I would have reported you the instant I discovered your secret. However, I have always believed women more capable than men credit them for. If they give them any credit at all.'

'I had hoped it would not be so evident,' I said quietly.

'It is evident to me. I fancy myself rather observant.'

'So I've noticed. Yet you are still here, despite the fact that this case appears to bore you. I wonder why that is.'

'I haven't formed an opinion yet. But it does indeed seem to be a rather dull one. I wonder...' Thoughtfully, he gazed at me and I realised that he had stayed to analyse me. I represented a curiosity.

'What made you change your identity?' he enquired.

'That's none of your concern, Mr Holmes.'

Suddenly, his expression changed as his *modus operandi* switched to analysis, and after a moment he seemed to reach a conclusion. 'I dare say that guilt might be the culprit.'

'What?'

'Women weren't allowed a higher education until very recently, and so you had to cut your hair and disguise yourself as a man to be able to study medicine. But the intriguing question remains: *Why* did you accept such drastic measures for a degree? Your accent is evident — you are a German who learned English in the Boston area. Harvard Medical School?'

I nodded once. My odd mix of American and British English and the German linguistic baggage were rather obvious.

'At first I thought you lived in East End, but I was wrong. You live in or very near St Giles.' He pointed a long finger to the splashes on my shoes and trousers. I wiped them every day before entering Guy's, but some bits always remained.

'The brown stains on your right index finger and thumb appear to be from harvesting parts of a medicinal plant.'

'Milk thistle,' I croaked.

'You probably treat the poor tree of charge, considering you use a herb that is certainly not used in hospitals, and the location in which you choose to live. London's worst rookery! You seem to have a tendency towards exaggerated philanthropy!' He flicked an eyebrow, his mouth lightly compressed, a mix of amusement and dismissal shining in his face.

'You don't care much about the appearance of your clothes,' he went on, ignoring my cold stare. 'They are a bit tattered on the sleeves and the collar, but surely not for lack of money. You have too little time! You probably have no tailor blind enough not to discover the details of your anatomy.'

I shot a nervous glance over his shoulder, assessing the distance to Gibson or any of his men. Mr Holmes waved at me impatiently, showing that my anxiety about being discovered by yet another man meant nothing to him. Fury roiled hot in my stomach.

He continued without pause. 'You have no one you can trust at your home, no housekeeper or maid to keep your secret. That forces you to do everything for yourself. In addition, there are your nightly excursions in the slums to treat your neighbours. You probably don't fancy sleep very much?' His voice was taunting now.

'I sleep four hours a day, on average.'

He continued in a dry, machine-like *rat-tat-tat*. 'You are very compassionate, even with the dead.' He pointed to the corpse between us. 'One of the few, typical female attitudes you exhibit, although in your case it's not a thing merely learned — there is a heaviness, a weight behind it. I must conclude that you feel guilty because someone you loved died. And now you want to help prevent that from happening to others. But you must fail repeatedly, because death and disease are natural. Considering your peculiar circumstances and your unconventional behaviour, I propose that you come from a poor home. Your father raised you after your mother died? Perhaps soon after your birth? Obviously, there hasn't been much female influence in your upbringing.'

Utterly taken aback by the triumph in his demeanour, I snarled, 'You are oversimplifying, Mr Holmes.' Rarely had anyone made me so angry, and only with effort could I keep my voice under control. 'It's not guilt that drives me. I would not have got so far if not for the passion I feel for medicine. My mother did die and I resent you for the pride you feel in deducing private details of my life. Details I do not wish to discuss with you!'

The man's gaze flickered a little.

'I met people like you at Harvard. Brilliant men, in need of constant stimulation of their mind, who see little else than their own work. Your brain runs in circles when not put to hard work, and boredom is your greatest torture.'

Mr Holmes's eyes sharpened.

'I saw those men use cocaine when there was nothing else at hand to tickle their minds. What about you, Mr Holmes?' His pupils dilated at the word "cocaine." I smiled. 'It doesn't help much, does it? Perhaps it is the cello that puts some order into that too chaotic mind of yours?'

I pointed to his left hand. 'The calluses on your fingertips. And how you hold the wrist of your right hand at times, as though you are holding a bow. But no, it's not the cello. The cello wants to be embraced. You prefer the violin — she can be held at a distance. You are a passionate man and you hide it well. But do you really believe that outsmarting everyone around you is an accomplishment?'

His expression was controlled and neutral, but his pupils were dilated to the maximum.

I rose to my feet, took a step forward, put my face close to his, and said softly, 'It feels like a stranger just ripped off all your clothes, doesn't it? Don't you dare dig into my private life again.' I tipped my hat, turned away, and left him in the grass.

2

❧❧❧

The two constables helped me wrap the corpse in a blanket and then place it onto the back of a waiting cart. As soon as the package was strapped down, they hastily put a safe distance between the stench and their insulted noses. When the younger of the two finished retching in the grass, I walked up to him, wiped off his hands with creosote, and gave him a brotherly clap on the shoulder.

Once I had disinfected everyone's hands, the inspector, Mr Holmes, and I stepped into a four-wheeler. Gibson snapped the door shut, and the carriage made a lurch. The Inspector sat, anticipation seeping from every pore. 'Well, it appears we don't need your services, Mr Holmes. The man died of a disease and toppled into the river. Wouldn't be the first, now would it?'

My blood began to boil. Gibson was referring to the unidentified men, women, and children found floating in the Thames at regular intervals, usually numbering more than fifty each month. Some had died of disease, others of pointy objects stuck in ribcages, throats, or elsewhere. When no one could spare the money for a funeral, the Thames surely took care of them.

'I fear it's far more complicated than that,' I grumbled.

'Excuse me? Please don't tell me the man was murdered, Dr Kronberg.' Gibson shot an amused stare at Holmes, who in turn smirked at no one in particular.

'There are only a few things we know for certain, Inspector. The man most likely died of cholera, and his corpse was floating in the river for one or two days. Both of which occurred upstream of London, and that,' I poked the air with my index finger, 'is highly unusual. Not to forget the restraint marks on his wrists. Or do you have a sound explanation for those?'

Gibson did not reply, only looked expectant, hoping perhaps that I would solve the case for him. Meanwhile, Holmes had refocused his absent-minded gaze as though he only now noticed our company.

Irritated by the two, I turned my face away to speak to the window instead. 'I will dissect the body upon arrival at Guy's and will hopefully learn what happened to the man. I'll send you a report tomorrow.'

'I will assist,' stated Mr Holmes with delight.

'Excuse me? I'm not in the habit of entertaining the public, and certainly won't allow a layman to attend a postmortem.'

'I believe you will.' His intense stare told me that I would indeed.

WE ARRIVED at Guy's after an hour of stale silence. At the porter's, I asked for a nurse, a cart and two helpers to transport the body to the dissecting department — a small red-brick building containing an antechamber equipped with several slabs of marble. We had the place to ourselves, as anatomical lessons were not given on Saturdays. That also meant I could disinfect the room with fumes of concentrated acid without having to discuss the issue with curious students.

Afterwards, I intended to prepare a report for the Home Office, stating, in essence, that there was no danger of cholera transmission through London's drinking water supply.

Gibson — not too eager to watch me cut up a floater — took his leave. I provided Mr Holmes and myself with an India rubber apron, gloves, and a mask. The last was a simple device, made of a fine, double-layered fabric, that I had contrived for such occasions. With the mask covering nose and mouth, dangerous airborne germs would not infect the man conducting the dissection or surgery — or, in my case, the woman. I felt nauseated at the thought that the man next to me knew my secret.

'Mr Holmes, may I recommend you visit a circus next time you want to see a curiosity?' I noted, regretting the snide remark instantly.

He coughed and replied, 'I guess I must apol—'

'Actually, this is not what worries me!' I slammed my hand onto the marble. 'I'm seriously considering blackmailing you. Unfortunately, you are rather sharp and my chances of winning such a game or even finding a rancid spot with which to taint your reputation are probably close to nil. So perhaps...' I groaned. Where the devil was my self-control? 'My apologies. Please assume I have been perfectly polite.'

I decided that I'd better keep my mouth shut. At least until my hands stopped trembling.

Mr Holmes, though, laughed heartily. 'I suppose your deceit is morally justifiable, although, if exposed, it would cause a public outcry. Fortunately, we both have the right to private judgement. Trust me in this, Dr Kronberg, exposing you to the police or anyone else is entirely unappealing to me.'

I peered over the edge of my mask and found his expression to be sincere enough. And yet, the stiffness of my spine would not disappear. To turn the attention to the matter at hand, I nodded at the corpse. We undid the blanket and hoisted the body onto the slab's polished surface.

With a pair of tweezers, I collected the fragments of flora and fauna caught on the body's clothes and hair, and placed them into a small bowl. Then I cut off the man's coat.

His shirt buttons did not show any grease prints, nor did the buttons of his trousers. I then proceeded to cut off the remainder of all his clothes and found restraint marks not only on his wrists, but also on his ankles, as well as needle punctures in the bend of the man's left elbow.

I pointed out the punctures and Holmes nodded, intent on scanning each square inch of newly revealed skin as I undressed the man in front of us.

'The punctures look professionally done, not like the holes they punch into people in those opium dens that also have cocaine solutions on the menu. Hum... He must have seen a medical doctor. Highly unusual,' I observed while picking up my largest knife.

I was uncertain about Holmes's nerves when it came to slicing apart human beings, so I kept half an eye on him while cutting a large Y into the man's torso, starting from the clavicles and extending down to the pubic bone. Holmes, though, seemed perfectly unmoved by the procedure, so I continued, sawing off the sternum and removing part of the thorax. The odour worsened significantly and reminded me once more that I would never get used to the stench of death.

While removing the lungs, the pressure I exerted on them resulted in an expulsion of pink froth from the corpse's nose and mouth. Grunting, I lifted the lungs into a bowl and cut them open.

'As I suspected — the man didn't drown,' remarked Mr Holmes upon the fact that the lungs were not filled with water.

'They contain only a small amount of dust and soot, supporting your assumption that the man spent most of his life in the countryside,' I said. Had he been a Londoner, his lungs would have been grey.

The number and size of the coagula inside the man's abdomen corroborated our assessment of the time of death.

That this was cholera in the final stage was as clear as day. In addition to the appearance of his skin, his liver was reduced and pale. His guts were empty for but a small amount of dirty greenish liquid.

All the organs went into separate bowls, leaving me panting and sweating. My physique was not ideal for a dissection, or, rather, I did not have the figure of a butcher. By now, my apron had taken on the function of a hothouse, and my hands inside my gloves felt like slippery fish.

Mr Holmes bent down low over the corpse and stared straight into the now empty cavity. Perhaps he found dissections entertaining.

Upon examining the man's mouth and eyes, I saw that his tongue was swollen and impressions of his teeth showed along its edges. I pushed at the remains of his eyelids. After a moment's consideration, I turned to Mr Holmes. 'What do you make of this?'

He gazed into the milky blue eyes with one pupil as small as a pinprick, the other spanning almost the entire iris.

'Poison, or possibly a head trauma?' he suggested.

'Hmm...' I answered and checked the man's skull again. But I could still not find any signs of violence.

I took up a smaller knife and made a cut along the frontal

hairline, then one along the crown down to his neck hairline. I peeled his scalp aside, and the upper half of his face down to his chin. My hands worked with precision, but my brain revolted. Skinning a human face was one more thing I knew I'd never get used to.

I picked up a saw and cut into the skull, then used a delicate chisel and a hammer to crack the bone along the grooves I had made. Great skill and caution were needed to cut only the bones and leave the nerve tissue undamaged.

The upper half of the skull came off like the top of a breakfast egg, revealing a brain that at first glance appeared normal. I extracted the right hemisphere and cut it into slices, took the magnifying glass from Mr Holmes's hand, and bent down over the brain sections. Small, liquid-filled lesions presented themselves.

'Odd!' I straightened up, tossing my tools aside. His magnifying glass produced a loud clonk on the slab. 'My apologies,' I muttered.

Pressing my knuckles onto the marble slab, I pushed all thoughts aside and let my gaze fly over the corpse, assembling bits of information in my mind, hoping a picture would form. What had I missed?

Impatiently, I yanked my gloves off and pressed my fingers into the bend of the man's elbow. The punctures felt stiffer than the surrounding tissue. I cut through them and pulled the skin apart. The vein was slightly infected.

'It seems as though the man had a needle inserted, which was left there for some time,' I said, rather baffled.

'That would make restraints necessary,' he concluded.

The man's stomach lay in a bowl next to me. I opened the organ and another surprise presented itself: half-digested bread and smoked fish, probably eel, swam merrily out of the opening.

'The man ate, though he shouldn't have had an appetite at

all during the final stage of cholera. And yet, he ate quite a few bites. I see no signs that he was forcibly fed, in either his mouth or oesophagus. Peculiarly, his stomach was cramped shut for probably two or three hours before his death. Although half-digested, none of the food made it into the small intestines. Why is that?'

My hands squeezed the slab hard as though a clue could be forced out that way. 'Mr Holmes, could it be possible after all that the man was pushed into the waterworks' trench?'

'I don't believe so. One might think a boat could have dropped him off, but the fish wouldn't have had time to eat all this,' he pointed to the corpse's face, 'before the body was discovered. Even if someone did go through the trouble of dragging the corpse with a boat for one or two days before dumping him in the trench, we would see very different marks on his body and clothes, from the ropes or hooks that would have held him to the vessel.'

'And if that someone planned to poison half of London with cholera, he would have made sure that the body was fresh,' I added. 'And several buckets of cholera-infected diarrhoea would have been much more effective and less suspicious than a body.'

'Precisely,' said Holmes.

A thought hit me. I almost slapped my forehead with my contaminated hands. I quickly washed them, took off my mask and apron, and said, 'Wait here,' before leaving in a rush. A few moments later I returned with a polished birch wood box, set it on one of the empty slabs, and extracted a stereo-microscope from it. I wiped its three lenses and both oculars with a silk handkerchief.

'May I introduce the best microscope you will ever set your eyes on? Or, rather, peer through,' I said enthusiastically. 'I found this one in Boston, although it's a German make. Its secret lies in the stacks of multiple lenses. I never came across a better one. It cost an arm and a leg,' I explained, as I extracted liquid from the man's vein. Holmes didn't react to the pun.

I placed a single drop of serum onto a glass slide and tipped a cover slip as thin as paper onto the drop to flatten the sample to a thin layer. Then I fastened the slide onto the holder just underneath the largest microscope lens and inserted a drop of immersion oil underneath. I aligned the small mirror at the bottom of the microscope towards the sun, peered through the oculars, and focused on the swirling particles.

'What resolution does it have?' asked Mr Holmes, sounding intrigued.

'It has a one-thousand-fold magnification, and I can see things as small as two micrometers.'

'Exceptional!' he whispered and scooted closer.

And there, in the microscope's circular field of view, swam peculiar cells shaped like minuscule tennis rackets only five micrometers long — bacteria that could kill every warm-blooded vertebrate. I moved aside to let him take a look.

'Germs!' he said, intrigued.

'Yes. It seems you were right again.' I smiled up at him.

'I never mentioned that possibility.'

'You did. You mentioned poison.' Upon his quizzical look, I added, 'Germs produce toxins. That's how they kill.'

'But...is cholera found in the bloodstream?'

'No,' I said, 'he didn't die of cholera. Although he had it quite severely, I believe he was already recovering. The food in his stomach indicates that. The deadly blow must have come from tetanus. But I don't know how he got infected. The needle punctures are only slightly inflamed, and don't show the typical appearance of a tetanus entry wound.'

Mr Holmes fell silent, mulled things over with a furrowed brow and narrowed eyes. I was almost done cleaning my tools when he muttered, 'I need to take that bowl with me,' indicating the collection of twigs, leaves, and beetles I had picked off the man's clothing.

'How good are you at identifying them?'

'I dare say the best.' He pulled off his gloves, apron, and mask, and I showed him how to disinfect his hands and the contents of the bowl he wanted to take with him. 'I suggest we meet Inspector Gibson at my residence tomorrow morning at nine.'

'Hmm...' I replied.

'Would that be a problem?'

'I'll consider it. I might deliver my report directly to him.' I avoided looking at Mr Holmes.

He turned to leave, but then seemed to think otherwise. 'I assume you will not tell me your real name?'

Aghast, I shook my head. 'Don't try to go behind my back to find it out.'

The thought must have crossed his mind, for he put a look of fake surprise on his face.

'Would you want me to go behind *your* back, to find out your address should I feel an urge to join the meeting of intellectuals tomorrow morning?'

He clicked his tongue and slapped his hand against the door frame. '221B Baker Street.'

3

I stepped off the omnibus and just managed to avoid a pile of horse manure on the pavement. The street sweeper stood nearby, leaning on his broom handle, chewing on something obviously ropy, and picking his teeth with blackened fingers. Such archaeological excavations exceeded even dissections at being unappetising.

I tossed him a coin, entered the eastern end of Regent's Park, and turned north. The bustling of the street behind me gradually dimmed, to be replaced by the quiet chatter of couples walking arm in arm and the grating chirps of sparrows.

After a few minutes, I reached 221B Baker Street. Like its neighbours, the three-storey house was built of red bricks, with its base looking as though it had been dipped in cream. It had large, white-framed windows and a smoked oak door. As my hand closed around the brass knocker, I wondered how much Holmes earned with that odd occupation of his. After a knock and a moment of waiting, a middle-aged house-keeper beckoned me in.

I watched my feet climb the stairs while thoughts swirled

around in my head like a swarm of mosquitoes. To me, Holmes was a magnet with north and south poles unified. He knew my secret and could, with a single statement, destroy my life. I wasn't quite certain whether avoiding or observing him was the safer tactic.

Upon reaching the landing, I finally lifted my gaze and noticed a small crater in the wall. I probed with my finger, then brushed the plaster off and peered through the hole. On the other side, I could see Gibson's head. Was this...a bullet hole?

Wondering who of Holmes's guests or clients had met a gruesome end on the stairwell, I knocked at the door.

'Enter,' said Holmes. I stepped into the room, and the world changed from polished and gleaming to utter chaos. The ceiling was decorated with stains, the spray pattern indicative of small explosions. Some spots looked as though acid had eaten into the plaster. I had noticed splotches on Holmes's hands yesterday but had not been able to identify them. Now I knew — the man was a lay scientist.

Enormous stacks of paper hid the desk, a chair, and most of the mantelpiece, where a knife stuck in the carved wood held a bunch of papers. On top of the marred ledge stood a photograph of a beautiful woman.

I apologised for being late. Gibson was now pacing the sitting room, hands clasped behind his back, chest and lower lip importantly stuck out. Holmes himself was smoking a pipe in an armchair by the fireplace, looking bored. A violin lay on the coffee table in front of him.

A small and timid chambermaid with hair the colour of dirty egg yolk served us tea and biscuits. She did not glance at anyone in the room. Slinking here and there, she seemed to go unnoticed by Gibson, who was lowering himself into the other armchair to receive his refreshments.

Holmes was giving Gibson the results of the dissection,

but finished without elaborating on the twigs and beetles, or offering any other thoughts on the case.

'Were you able to identify the man, Inspector?' I enquired.

Annoyed, he shook his head. 'I already told Mr Holmes I'm afraid it will be entirely impossible. He didn't have any papers on him and no one who fits his description has been reported missing. I will not waste my time investigating this case. I hope you agree, Mr Holmes.'

Holmes nodded without looking up, and Gibson heaved himself off the chair with a satisfied smile.

I handed Gibson my report, and he merely nodded. 'Dr Kronberg,' he said, and took his leave.

'That was awkward,' I said. 'Why was he even here?'

'He enjoys the biscuits.'

'Coming here was a waste of time.' I turned and grabbed the doorknob, then stopped as a thought hit me. I leant my back against the door frame. 'Interesting.'

Mr Holmes blinked, apparently surprised to see that I was still there.

'Is there anything else, Dr Kronberg?' His voice was monotonous.

'Gibson is wrong, you know it, and yet you didn't say anything,' I answered. Holmes raised one eyebrow.

'May I ask you a question?' I produced a warm smile. 'Actually two. Did I miss anything of importance owing to my late arrival?' He shook his head once. 'The second question is: did you find anything of interest in the bowl you took home yesterday?'

'It was full of insects, leaves, and dirt. Highly interesting.' He yawned.

His gaze followed mine as I looked at the violin and said, 'She is on top of the breadcrumbs — you played her before Gibson came in. Are you on a case at present?'

He narrowed his eyes and I saw him getting ready for combat.

'What amused you about the maid?' he asked calmly.

'Ah, a diversion. Well, then. I was wondering why she was so extremely shy. Whether it could be her inexperience, or a problem she has with you. The fact that I found myself wondering about it at all, was, well... amusing.'

'Amusing?'

'Mr Holmes, you are — as per your own definition — highly observant. Yet you want me to believe that you don't know the impression you leave on others?'

'I have a theory, but as I am involved, my judgement is not entirely unbiased.'

'You scare people. Even shallow foozlers like Gibson.' I stated simply. He could digest it as he pleased. But Holmes's response surprised me — he chuckled.

Accidentally, I cast a look at the woman on the mantelpiece.

'Another theory I would like to hear,' he said, and I knew he had put me under the microscope the moment I entered his rooms.

Seeing my startled expression, he produced a flood of explanations. 'I noticed you glancing around as you entered. You looked rather taken aback. What a contrast to that neat staircase, isn't it? My piles of papers and the spots on the walls and ceiling amused you. I could almost see the pictures of explosive experiments forming in your head. Very refreshing, indeed! Then you discovered the photograph,' he pointed to the woman's picture, 'and your eyes lingered there for two seconds. You have formed an opinion.'

He put his hands back in his lap and sat there, relaxed, while monitoring his surroundings without the slightest movement of his head. The man had very long antennae indeed.

'I am curious, Mr Holmes — if you don't want to involve me in this case, why not simply ask me to leave? Another thing I was just wondering was whether you've ever met anyone able to avoid your analytical skills. Someone who could observe you well enough and avoid being analysed by you. Without being obvious, I mean.'

'You are evading my question.' Still with that calm voice.

I started wondering what could possibly rattle his composure.

'What question? I must have forgotten it,' I mumbled and then, seeing him pointing his chin at the photograph, I said softly, 'Your weak spot.'

At that, he pulled the corners of his mouth down. 'You are reading Dr Watson. How disappointing,' he announced, and slapped his armrest.

That was an odd answer. In my mind I scanned through the last publications I had read, but couldn't remember any by Watson and colleagues. Holmes noticed my confusion.

'Are you not reading the papers?' he enquired, a little perplexed.

'Er... No, not really. What does that have to do with her?' I waved my hand at the picture.

'If you had read my friend's stories, you would know who Irene Adler is.'

'Your friend writes stories about your romantic life in the newspapers? Is he the one you shot?' I pointed at the hole in the wall.

'I did not shoot him. Or *anybody*, yet. Although, I *will* put a hole in his head should he ever dare—'

'Oh, it's Dr Watson you live with!' I had noticed a some-what worn-looking coat on a hook by the door. It was made to fit a stocky man of approximately my height. Also, the two armchairs appeared to be regularly used. I could not quite imagine Holmes receiving visitors every day and openly inviting them to wear out his furniture. Probably his distressed customers preferred to pace the room, and ruin the carpet instead.

After a moment of sizing me up, Holmes grumbled, 'He lives with his new wife now. You are evading my question again.'

I was quite enjoying our banter. And I had a plan. 'You are rather impatient, Mr Holmes. May I?' I asked, gingerly picking up the picture. He didn't look too happy but let me proceed, and I started pacing his sitting room.

'There are few pictures on the walls and they are almost completely hidden behind that chaos of yours. I should assume they were hung there before you moved in and are of no importance to you.' I pushed at the frame of a particularly ugly one, and saw that the wallpaper behind it was darkened. 'No need to answer that.' I continued. 'All that is in sharp contrast to this picture of her. She is the only photograph on the mantelpiece. Possibly because you don't know how to drive a nail into the wall?'

A frown on Holmes's face indicated that he did indeed know how to use a hammer. Good for him. 'There is your collection of knick-knacks littering mantelpiece. If she were insignificant, she would be hidden, at least partially. But there she is, in full view. However, she is not someone you are fond of, because you never take her off her place. Although I'm not entirely sure you would ever do such a thing, even if you were fond of her.'

Holmes appeared highly alert now and I, not knowing whether he could sense my plan, put a little more distance between us while continuing my explanation. 'The frame and the glass appear to be free of fingerprints. I guess she was touched once to be put there. The maid cleans your rooms daily, but not very thoroughly, mostly because she doesn't dare touch your personal belongings.'

I reached a window close to the fireplace, opened it and pulled the curtain aside. I coughed — the room was stuffy with pipe smoke — and took a good lungful of fresh air. Inwardly, I was vibrating with excitement and foreboding — I was about to step onto a rather fragile tightrope.

'There is only one possible explanation, Mr Holmes. You dislike the woman, yet you keep her photograph. That can only mean that you adore her in a queer way. Considering what I learned about you yesterday, I conclude that she outwitted you. You are convinced you are the smartest man alive, and being outwitted by a woman was more than unacceptable to you. This is your greatest conceit and your weakest spot. You should get rid of it.'

With these last words, my hand shot out of the window. Holmes inhaled a hiss.

'For Christ's sake!' he huffed, as I drew my hand back in, and placed her picture gently on the windowsill.

'Now, would you be so kind as to tell me what you think about the Hampton man's death, Mr Holmes?' I asked.

'There isn't much to think,' he snarled, stood, and picked up Irene. 'All that's needed is but a simple calculation: the maximum distance the man could have floated was thirty miles. He entered the Thames as a corpse, which means he was close to death before he even got to the river. He can only have contracted cholera in a densely populated place with a lack of hygiene, and he could not have walked very far. It follows that he must have been close to a village or city. There is only one place that fits these facts like a glove fits the hand!'

'And which place would that be?'

He ignored me and placed the photograph back on the mantelpiece.

'I wonder why you are so observant,' he muttered after a moment. I opened my mouth to reply, but he held up his hand. 'Of course! You are behind the veil. You are the one no one sees but who must perceive everything. You must be observant to protect your life in disguise.'

His back still towards me, he asked, 'Would you accompany me to Chertsey Meads?'

'Excuse me?'

'Do I have to repeat the question?' He turned around.

'Is that a drinking hall?' I joked.

'It is a wetland.'

I took my time to find the right words. 'I must confess I feel honoured by your invitation, although I am not sure why I would be. I also have the feeling that the main reason for your invitation is to study me a little longer. That irks me, because I am not a curiosity. And your constant probing of my brain is highly annoying.' I saw him pulling his eyebrows together and asked, 'Why should I come with you, Mr Holmes?'

The corners of his mouth twitched in a hint of a smug smile. 'Because you are enjoying yourself, and there is nothing at the moment you would like to do more than to probe *my* brain a little while longer.'

4

We sat on the train to Chertsey and the landscape whizzed past unnoticed. To my surprise, I enjoyed myself as we discussed the Whitechapel murders. The topic itself, though, was rather unpleasant. Jack the Ripper had killed at least six women. He had cut their throats, sliced their abdomens open, draped their intestines over both their shoulders, and had taken souvenirs with him — usually the victim's uterus.

To say that Holmes had a low opinion of the Yard's efforts would be an understatement. 'Every time I receive a telegram from the police, the bodies have already been taken away to the morgue,' he exclaimed. 'The staff have extracted organs and sold them as surgical specimens. Of course, they never remember what they took, and what had already been taken! I have serious doubts that this series of murders will ever be solved and the culprit found. The incompetence of the responsible investigators, the coroner, and the medical staff, along with the sheer number of false witnesses and all the misinformation spread by the newspapers render all investigations futile!'

He looked rather ruffled, with his mouth compressed and his hands knuckling the seat.

Gazing out the window, I sorted through my mind trying to find the right words. 'Owing to my occupation, I come across a rather large number of stab wounds,' I said, turning back to him. 'One of the peculiar things I've noticed is that almost all the women with knife wounds in their lower abdomen were victims of attempted rape. And of those who survive this kind of attack, all report that the rapist used a knife because he was unable to penetrate them. He was unable to produce an erection. Doesn't that add a very different angle to the Ripper's motives?'

Holmes leant back in his seat and stared out of the window. After several long minutes, he turned his face back to me and said, 'The Ripper used several prostitutes, indicating a high sexual drive. If he indeed was never able to finish a sexual act, he must have accumulated a great amount of frustration.'

Passengers close by started to cough and wag their fingers at us. Some took their children by the hand and left the waggon. Holmes ignored their protests and I had my hand over my mouth to hide my grin, but my eyes betrayed me. He noticed my amusement and shot me an indignant glance.

'My sincere apologies, Mr Holmes. I couldn't help but think that any other man,' I leant forward and lowered my voice, 'would feel awkward saying that straight into a woman's face.'

'As what shall I treat you, then? Male or female?' he said sharply, which resulted in the full attention of the remaining passengers.

'I want to be treated with respect, and you did that. Thank you,' I said. There was a long moment of silence, both of us measuring the other until some kind of common ground seemed to be reached.

'The fact that one victim was not enough, that he needed to kill more, also tells us a lot about the murderer,' I added quietly.

'He craves power,' noted Holmes.

'He has none otherwise?'

'Perhaps. Hm... Everyone hunts the bird of prey. But what if the mouse is the culprit?' His excitement soon dissolved into thoughtfulness as he recommenced staring out the window. The long, silent stretches that interrupted our conversation did not feel uncomfortable. Neither of us liked small talk.

CHERTSEY WAS a neat little town with old houses, small front yards, and the occasional goat or cat passing by, wondering who the deuce these two intruders were.

'Ah!' exhaled Holmes, disappointed, as we reached the road flanking the wetland. We had expected to find footprints on dirt roads, but the street was cobblestoned. He bent low at the sides of the narrow street, and strained his eyes to identify potential traces of the Hampton man's activities. Occasionally he was on all fours, almost touching the dirt with his nose, his magnifying glass at the ready.

Meanwhile, I scanned the meadow. The wind moved the grass in waves and the sun painted flickering lights on their tips. The gentle movement revealed faint criss-crossing patterns where hare and deer must have passed. I bent down and investigated the base of the grass and the small tunnels shaped by animals foraging for food. Our progress was depressingly slow and, at that point, without results.

When I got impatient and excused myself, Holmes only grunted in response.

At a nearby willow, I took off my shoes and socks, rolled

up my trousers and sleeves, and climbed up the tree. A gap in the foliage allowed a grand view of the whole of Chertsey Meads. I spotted Holmes, yet again on all fours. The man was quite persistent. Larks were blaring and a harrier flapped its long, black-tipped wings, swaying across the river.

Then I saw it: Among the faint animal tracks was one with grass broken higher up on the stakes. Only a large animal could have produced that. I stuck two fingers into my mouth and blew hard.

Holmes stood erect and looked around. It seemed as though he had just noticed my disappearance. I whistled again and he spotted me.

'Another twenty-five yards, Mr Holmes!' I yelled through the funnel of my hands. Instantly, Holmes turned and walked the recommended distance. He inspected the ground and the grass for a moment, cried out in surprise, and darted off towards the Thames.

I climbed down, grabbed my shoes and socks, and took a shortcut to the other end of the trail. As a child, I'd learned that running barefooted through a wetland can cause sharp grass to cut in deep between the toes. So I stomped instead, hoping Holmes wouldn't see me.

The river clucked quietly and reed warblers ranted at each other. I was careful not to tread on the trail, but I could already see that someone had walked here. Right next to the river, the grass and reeds were bent across an area of about two by four yards. He must have rested there. Suddenly, I remembered the Hampton man's shoes. Holmes had shown them to me. But the prints were not identical to the soles I had seen.

'Wait!' cautioned Holmes when he saw me taking a step towards the river's edge.

He examined the trodden place for only a minute or so and then said, 'As expected.'

'And *what* did you expect?'

'The Hampton man walked — or, rather, hobbled — only half the distance through the meads. He was accompanied by Mr Big Boots.' Holmes pointed to the ground next to him. There in the mud were the clear footprints I had seen already. The ones with the holes at the heels were missing.

'He carried him,' I noted.

'Yes. And here,' he pointed again, 'he laid him down.'

There was a faint elongated impression. It was of a size to fit the Hampton man's body.

'The two must have been friends,' he stated and, seeing my quizzical expression, he explained, 'Big Boots carried him, and there are no signs of a fight. This allows us to make an assumption only. But here is the simple proof.' He pointed to the impression of buttocks right next to the longish dent. 'The Hampton man died while resting his head in his friend's lap!'

He contemplated for two seconds, stated that there was nothing more to be learned there, and traced his steps back to the road, unsuccessfully searching for more traces of the two men's presence.

We walked back into Chertsey. Holmes's plan was to enquire at the local inn whether anyone had seen the two.

We entered a small stone house with *The Meads Inn* painted in neat red letters over the entrance door. The inn itself consisted of a tiny room with a mawkish interior design. A woman who was probably interior decorator and the owner's wife, beckoned us in. Her eyelids and hands were flapping in unison, probably intended to appear inviting.

Holmes steered us towards a table. We ordered stew and beer and, as the woman set our meal down in front of us, he let a sovereign spin on the polished wood.

'We are looking for two men who passed through Chertsey Meads the day before yesterday. One was more than six feet and eight inches tall, and probably supporting the other, a man who was seriously ill, unusually pale, undernourished, and almost a head shorter than his friend. Both were dressed poorly. Have you seen them, by any chance?'

The woman flinched. She didn't even look at the money that swirled so promisingly before her eyes.

I threw her an apologetic glance. Holmes hadn't introduced us.

'My apologies, ma'am. I am Dr Anton Kronberg and this is Mr Sherlock Holmes. We are investigating a crime and would be ever so grateful if you could help us.'

Her expression didn't soften the least.

'Haven't seen nuffink!' she said abruptly, turned around, and disappeared into the kitchen.

'That went well,' I mumbled, leaning over my bowl and shovelling hot stew into my mouth.

Holmes only smiled a little, then turned his attention to his food, and ate it merrily.

'How could you know how tall Big Boots was? By the size of his shoes?' I asked.

'And stride length.'

'Ah.' I thought about that for a while and added, 'You can calculate that although Big Boots had to support the Hampton man? Wouldn't his stride be shorter owing to the effort?'

Holmes talked to his stew. 'It would be, but in this case, the strain did not appear to be significant. When the Hampton man leaned on Big Boots, the latter didn't show a sideways tilt of his heels to counteract the force. And we know the Hampton man was light. Big Boots's stride length didn't change in the least even as he picked up his friend and carried him. All these facts indicate that he was in rather good health, tall and strong.'

My brain absorbed the information like a hungry cat the milk.

After we had drained our beer, he announced that he wanted to take his leave at once.

The woman hurried back to us, we paid, and Holmes asked casually, 'You had a burglary?'

She stopped in her tracks. 'Why, yes! How did ya know?'

Holmes pointed towards the window. The sash was missing, probably taken out for repair. I had noticed it as we came in, but hadn't thought of a crime, for a pub's window panes are chronically threatened by its clientele.

'Yes...yes...two days ago,' she stammered.

'What has been taken?'

'Food, mostly, and the oil lamp from over the door,' she said, pointing to the exit.

'What about clothes?' I asked. She stumbled backwards, almost bumping into the wall.

'How did ya... My husband's coat...but how could ya...'

'It is but a simple observation of—' I elbowed Holmes to interrupt his explanation. The woman was shocked enough and there was no need to pour more information into her already stunned brain.

'Did the burglar leave something behind?' he asked with an annoyed sideways glance at me.

'What do ya mean?' she said, and noticing Holmes's impatient look, she added: 'No, he hasn't left nuffink.'

'Did you seen him?' I asked.

'Of course I didn't!' she said and stomped back into the kitchen.

As MADE our way back to the station I asked Holmes

whether he had also got the impression the woman was hiding something.

He snorted. 'Who isn't?'

As we took our seats on the train back to London, he asked, 'Is it possible to contract tetanus without an infected wound?'

'Actually, it is. I was thinking about that last night. He could have got tetanus from eating bad or dirty meat. I have seen people who've eaten cats, dogs, and rats. When one hasn't the patience, or wood enough to fully cook the meat, one will likely contract whatever disease the animal had.'

Holmes's eyes glazed over, and he fell silent for a long time. We had almost reached London when he said, 'We have to find Big Boots. Could he have contracted cholera, too?'

'Not necessarily.' I noticed the glint of hope in Holmes's eyes fading. 'Would a second cholera victim come in handy to solve the case?'

He mirrored my stare and answered, 'Without Big Boots, it is unlikely I will ever solve the case. There is not enough information.'

After another long and silent stretch, I said, 'Mr Holmes, I'm rather confused. Two men take a walk together to the Thames. One dies of tetanus while having cholera in the final stage, and is thrown into the river. The same one having restraint marks on his wrists and ankles. Both men steal food and a coat, and hours later the coat is thrown into the water together with the man who wore it. This makes absolutely no sense.'

'Hmm...' answered Holmes. And that was the last word he spoke until we parted in London.

5

Merely a week after the Hampton incident, I found a man in my ward, lying on the floor in silent agony. His spine was arched far back, his arms pulled to his body, fists clenched, and feet curled inward. In the short moment it took me to rush up to him, I saw that it was too late. All I could do was kneel at his side, take his fist in my hand, and wait for the seizure to release its grip.

Patients who were strong enough propped themselves up on their cots for a better view. Anxious muttering began to fill the room, mingling with anger and pity.

The man stilled, and faint vibrations began to run through all the muscles in his tense body. His facial features were stretched into a devilish grin and his eyes had rolled far back in his skull. I placed my other hand on his chest. His heart was still beating, but the muscle spasms arrested his breathing.

'The pain will go away,' I whispered.

His fluttering heart didn't accept its fate. But only a minute later, it too ceased moving. No one in the ward spoke. The presence of death had sealed their lips. Only a quiet cough, the rustling of blankets, and the whimpering of a child cut through the void.

This was one of the hardest things for me. To acknowledge defeat, concede to the inevitable, and let go a life that had been entrusted to me. Strangely enough, when all was over, and silence fell, there was a short moment of deepest peace. As though Death touched my shoulder to salute an old acquaintance.

I pulled a clean sheet over the body, and left the ward to find someone who might know the man's identity. For I could only guess at who might dump a dying man on the cold floor of my ward. I spotted the old porter, Mr Osburn, pacing the corridor. When he saw me, he waved both arms and came running.

'Do *you* know who did this?' I pointed behind me.

'He's dead, isn't he?' he said anxiously, peeking around me and through the door.

'Yes, he died. Did you know him?'

'Oh, no!' said Osburn, shaking his head, his large ears almost flapping. 'Didn't know him. Found him on the street, just in front of the gate.'

'What? And you dumped him here without informing me? Are you mad?'

His eyes flared, then he dropped his gaze, his posture slumped, and he stammered, 'Am sorry, am sorry, I didn't know what to do. I found him by the gates, knew his was dying, and...and so I...I...brought him in here. And Billy from the disinfectors helped carrying him, and we didn't see no doctor and no nurses and didn't know what to do, and I didn't find no one, all the time thinking about that poor man dying. And then I come back and you were here and...and... He was dead.'

I inhaled a deep breath, and made myself say, 'Thank you, Mr Osburn. Did you see who dropped him off?'

He eyed me from below his lashes, and immediately dropped his gaze again. He shook his head.

'Are you sure? Perhaps you heard something before you found him?"

He began pulling an earlobe. Wagged his head, and said, 'Hum.'

After a long moment, he pulled himself up a little, and said, 'Now that you mention it, believe I heard the crack of a whip. I'm quite sure. There was the whinnying of a horse, just a moment afore I heard the gasping of a man. That man, you know, and then I found him. And then brought him here.'

I thanked him again and he mumbled something in return, then hobbled back to his porter house.

Before I returned to my patients, I asked a nurse to arrange the transport of the body to the anatomy lecture hall and to announce a presentation at four o'clock for students of medicine and bacteriology.

THE CONTORTED CORPSE lay atop a marble slab in the centre of the hall and stuck out like a sore navel. Behind it, tiers of horseshoe benches rose from floor to ceiling. The anatomical theatre was packed. Murmurs and the scraping of feet filled the air. Most of the young men were familiar to me, and the few new ones in the front rows would soon push back.

I coughed, and all faces turned toward me. The ones who knew the rules elbowed the new students who were about to light their cigarettes or pipes, resulting in a moment of confusion and muttering.

'Ladies and gentlemen!' I announced. It was a bold joke, for only male students were admitted, not to mention only male lecturers. After a short while, the guffawing ceased and the theatre fell quiet. My reputation was such that the young men obeyed the few rules I set: no talking and no smoking, or they would have to leave at once. But they also knew that there wouldn't be a dull moment in the next two hours.

'Today around noon, this man was found by the entrance gates. He had severe muscle spasms and was unable to walk. He was brought to my ward and died within minutes. Does anyone here have an idea as to the cause of his death?'

After a moment, a new student from the front row squared his shoulders and cried, 'Tetanus!'

As expected.

I shook my head and smiled. 'You might be wrong there.'

His face fell. 'With all due respect, Dr Kronberg—'

'I do hope so, Mister, but I fear you forgot to introduce yourself.'

'My name is Wallace McFadin.'

'A Scot! Very well, then! I like your music, Mr McFadin. Do you play the bagpipes well?'

'Er... I'm... I don't play bagpipes.'

'But you are Scottish?'

'Yes, I am.' His cheeks were acquiring a reddish glow.

'So if you are a Scot, why don't you play the bagpipes? And where, if I may ask, is your kilt?'

'That is conjecture, if not outright prejudice!' He slammed his knuckles on the table in front of him.

'Precisely,' I said, and saw that I had lost him. 'My apologies, Mr McFadin, I used you for a demonstration. When you meet a Scot, he doesn't necessarily play the bagpipes. The same is true for Mr Unknown here.' I pointed to the man on the slab. 'He died while exhibiting severe muscle spasms. You can see all the typical tetanus symptoms, including the remarkable devilish grin.'

Touching the man's cold cheek, I wondered how many of my students felt repelled, how many pitied the man, how many were amused by his shocking appearance. I looked back at them and continued. 'But does that necessarily mean that he died from tetanus? No, it does not! I urge everyone in this room to be cautious and to refrain from allowing limited knowledge to mask our senses. Just because we *think* it must have been tetanus that killed the man, doesn't necessarily mean this is indeed the case. Preconception prohibits learning! Only after we have learned all there is to learn, after we have studied and observed, only then can we draw our conclusions. And do not expect to always find an answer to your questions. If you have done your very best and still cannot find an explanation, it is acceptable and honourable to say, "I do not know."'

Several students were looking a bit perplexed now. I knew they had learned that superiority went hand in hand with practising medicine. This, in my opinion, was all rubbish.

'You must see yourselves as scientists. And science is a work in progress. As is learning. You are solving a bacterial crime, gentlemen! I know that many of your lecturers teach you to view the person you are dissecting as a subject. It is easier to slice apart a thing than a human being. But if you do so, you are ignoring important facts. The man could have died of an infectious disease, which makes him a human being with a significant history. A history that you must reveal! How else can you identify the causative agent, and thus aid in the prevention of further infections? Read up on Dr Snow's reports on the last cholera outbreak and how he found the pump on Broad Street as the vector of transmission. The man investigated the *history* of the cholera fatalities, and only that allowed him to successfully prevent any further spreading of the disease. When you wake up in the morning — every morning! — I want you to think of the only thing we know for sure, which is that, in fact, we know very little. After you have done so, throw away one of your favourite preconceptions.'

McFadin's colour faded back to a normal shade and he seemed even a little proud to have been of such excellent service. Everyone was glued to my lips, and the show could begin.

'Now, if you please...' I waved them forward. That was unusual for most anatomical demonstrations. Normally, students were asked to keep a respectful distance. Not during my lessons, however. I wanted them to observe closely, though I had to keep an eye on the faint-hearted ones. They usually fared better when given a task, rather than asked to merely watch. So far, however, everyone looked brave. 'Now tell me, what do you observe?'

Several students answered.

'His clothes are dirty and old.'

'He is thin.'

'He is poor.'

'He has brown hair.'

'He is about forty years old.'

'His body is distorted.'

I interrupted. 'Thank you very much! We can safely assume that the man was poor, has brown hair, and was probably thirty years old. Poverty often makes one look older than one really is. And his body is distorted. Can anyone say where the man came from?'

They all shook their heads.

'Exactly. So far, we can't tell.' I searched his pockets and found them to be empty, then fetched a pair of scissors and cut away trousers, shirt, and underwear. I took off his boots, then placed everything on the floor.

'What can we see now?' I asked the group.

'He is naked!' someone shouted. We all had a good laugh.

'Excellent observation! I should have asked my question a little differently. What can we *not* see?'

That was always the hardest: detecting those things that were missing. As expected, everyone looked clueless.

'How do people typically contract tetanus?' I hinted.

'Through dirt in a deep wound,' someone replied.

'Do you see any?' I asked.

The young men craned their necks and after a while, shook their heads.

'Shall we turn him?' We did, but there were no wounds on his back, either.

'How else can tetanus enter the body?' No one answered, so I did. 'You could eat an animal that has tetanus, for example.'

Suddenly, I remembered the Hampton man. I examined this man's wrists and ankles but found no restraint marks. Then I checked the bends of both elbows — again nothing. The students looked at me enquiringly.

'What else could produce these symptoms?'

Silence. Well, most of them hadn't yet had toxicology, so I answered my own question again. 'The alkaloid of the strychnos tree, commonly known as strychnine. It killed Alexander the Great, for example.'

Murmurs filled the room and I waited for silence before I continued. 'To be able to distinguish between these two, we have to open the man.'

I moved the table with my utensils closer to the slab. As expected, the new students pushed farther back the moment I took my largest knife and ran it through the corpse's skin.

I could not find any infected areas in his gastrointestinal tract, but his heart had a swollen, dark — almost black — area. I cut it open and held it to my nose. It stank. I couldn't explain to my students how tetanus had got into the man's heart. We were all mystified. I opened the cranium, sliced the hemispheres into sections, and found the typical liquid-filled lesions that tetanus can produce, but not strychnine. I straightened up then and said, 'It appears that Scots do play the bagpipes after all.'

McFadin grinned back at me.

When the lesson was over, I sent a wire to Holmes, wrapped the boots and clothes in waxed paper, and left for home.

6

I walked along the buzzing streets, trying to avoid collisions with other pedestrians. Street vendors advertised their goods, and a variety of odours wafted through the heavy summer evening air — fish, pastries, smoke, blood, urine, and stale sweat. I bought an eel pie and ate it while walking, the package for Holmes clamped under my arm.

The direct way home was a three-mile journey, which I usually did not take. I seldom walked or rode the same route on two consecutive days. It was my way to disconnect my two lives — the male and the female. If anyone wanted to follow me from Guy's to my home, they would have a hard time doing so.

When the weather permitted, I chose to walk. On other days I took an omnibus or a hansom cab to some place close to Bow Street.

The day was dry and sunny, a good evening for a stroll. I passed over London Bridge, turned left onto Upper Thames Street and walked to Blackfriars Bridge, crossed the river a second time, then on to Stamford, and over the Thames again at Waterloo Bridge, passed by the Strand and an eating house where I sometimes took supper, walked along Charles Street, and at last on to Bow Street.

At the back door of the cobbler's, I made my way up a narrow staircase, careful not to bump my head on the low ceiling beam at the very top of the stairs, and then turned into a dark corridor just beneath the attic.

I unlocked the door at the far end and entered a tiny, windowless room. Very conveniently, my landlady had poor eyesight and it was easy to make her believe that I used the room as storage for costumes. I had told her that at odd times my clients or I would enter, pick out a dress, and leave. And because these few possessions represented my entire riches — which I could not afford to lose — she allowed me the privilege of installing an additional lock, to which only I would have the key. It was an unusual arrangement, but she needed the extra shilling I paid her each week.

I unlocked the door, struck a match, and lit an oil lamp. Once inside my secret dressing chamber, I slid the bolt home, and went to the wardrobe. Its door creaked open, and the looking glass affixed inside revealed a view of Dr Anton Kronberg, respectable member of the medical establishment, dressed in a sand-coloured cotton shirt, cotton trousers of a darker shade, and patent leather shoes. His hair was slicked back with Macassar oil. Well educated, distinguished, and peculiarly delicate. A few of the nurses at Guy's found him quite handsome.

What a waste.

I unbuttoned my shirt, took it off, and draped it over a hanger, then pulled off my shoes, trousers, and stockings. My fingers probed inside the wrappings around my chest until one end of the bandages was found and I could free my compressed bosom. While rolling the cotton strip into a ball, the red stripes on my breasts slowly paled.

I pulled down my drawers, and checked that the seams

around a roll of stockings I had sewn into the crotch were intact. I placed them onto a shelf next to my fake cock — a contraption made of fine calf leather attached to a harness I could sling around my hips. A narrow tube was sewn into the cock, its other end attached to a small water-filled pouch. I rarely used it. Perhaps once every two months, especially when a new colleague was around and glanced at my hairless chin a little too intensely for my comfort. Then I would make an effort to follow him to the restrooms, clap him on the shoulder with all my manly might, position myself two or three urinals away from him, and let a noisy stream of liquid hit the porcelain bowl, which effectively drowned any and all doubts about my sex before they had an opportunity to grow. The artificial cock appeared authentic enough as long as no one looked too closely — and no man in his right mind would ever dare do such a thing.

I gazed at my naked body and let the fact sink in that I was yet again a woman. Every morning I shed my female self and made myself believe I was a man. To me, it was the only way not to be afraid. I had no time for fear when I was at work. Rather, I had no time for fear at all. But this was more naivete than courage. If my identity were revealed, I would simply start a new life elsewhere. That's what I tried to make myself believe. But one part of my consciousness kept telling me how hard it would be to let go of all I had accomplished.

I rarely listened.

The left-hand side of my wardrobe contained all things female. I pulled on a bodice, stockings, a petticoat, and a simple dark linen dress. A scarf around my head concealed my rather short hair. All in all, I wasn't much to look at. But as soon as I went down to the streets, it felt as though I'd thrown myself onto the market for sexual reproduction. Men I walked past would reach out almost unintentionally just to brush my shoulder or waist. As a woman, a lot more obstacles were thrown in my way.

From Bow Street, I turned north and walked the few blocks to my small flat in Endell Street, St Giles — the worst rookery in the British Empire.

London was a monster with many heads — or faces, to be more precise. One could stroll down a clean and busy street, but take a wrong turn and one would disappear into a maze of dark and filthy alleys that were home to millions of rats the size of a cabbage. Rodents throve in the slums more than any other creature. They were the only inhabitants who always had enough to eat, be it fermenting cabbage, faeces, or cadavers — both animal and human. Life was hard in the slums. Clean water was a rare commodity, as were food, shelter, warmth in winter, clothes — basically anything that would make life acceptable. An uninitiated visitor would likely emerge unburdened of all his money, perhaps even of all his clothes. If he emerged at all.

At the other end of the scale were the tranquil and clean upper-class areas. Beautifully dressed and well-behaved ladies and gentlemen could stroll through the parks without being bothered by the poor and dirty. There, even the trees and bushes were well groomed. People had enough to eat, though their servants often did not.

Every day, my way to and from Guy's Hospital took me through these contrasting districts. Every day, I saw the transformation of a city, from beautiful villas to filthy bottom-of-the-pit hovels where potato sacks and battered hats served as replacements for missing window panes.

And so also did I transform, from the fake male bacteriologist and epidemiologist Anton Kronberg to Anna Kronberg — fake widow and fake medical nurse. I knew that changing identities had its risks, but I was glad to take them. In Boston, I had lived as Anton only, and after three years my own body became a stranger to me. The lack of a penis seemed worrying, and breasts useless, ugly appendages. So much so that I hid even at night. After many weeks of tightly bandaging my chest, I got a breast infection that threw me down with a high fever and excruciating pain. I spent a week in bed, naked. After that, I would not hide my female identity for much longer than a day. I needed to be Anna, to not lose myself.

To AVOID a meeting with my landlady, I ran up the creaking stairs to my apartment and slammed the door shut before she had opened hers. The stench in the hallway told me she'd had too much gin and too little time to discard the contents of her chamber pots. Almost every day, I was glad they had no children. The crying of neglected youngsters on top of their shouting wars would have been unbearable.

I cut bread and cheese, lit the stove to make tea, and then ate my sandwich standing at the open window and listening to the odd mix of drunkard sing-song, children's play, dog yowls, and laughter. There was life here, and I found it so much more interesting and complex than that of the higher classes.

Having no time to linger, I fetched a bucket and walked down to the street to fetch water from a pump. Back in the room, I washed the Macassar oil out of my hair and the dissection odour from my body. As I owned only one outfit that might be considered appropriate for a lady of the upper middle class, there wasn't much thinking to be done on what the deuce I should wear. I put on a camisole and laced my corset, yanked up my petticoats and pulled my dark blue silk dress over all those useless layers.

I looked myself over in the glass on the wall, and saw a woman I barely recognised. There were too many sharp angles on me to be considered pretty. But those I was used to. Expensive fabric poured from my shoulders down to ankles stuck in tightly laced boots. My black velvet hat was adorned with a single raven feather, shimmering blue and violet in the evening sun. Black curls peeked out, almost reaching my chin. My short hair was definitely too progressive and onlookers might think me to be on my way to a Suffragettes' meeting. Everything about my face screamed oddity. The chin was set too boldly, my eyes were too determined, my nose too long. As a woman, I looked too masculine and, as a man, too feminine.

My face fell. I didn't have much time left. A black-haired man in his thirties or forties without even having the hint of a beard, simply did not exist. With luck, I could perhaps go on with this charade for another ten years. But what would I do then? How could I possibly live without science?

With a growl, I kicked the wall, then snatched the package for Holmes off the table, took a small handbag, and started south. Just as I turned a corner, I heard the *flap flap flap* of naked feet on the pavement behind me, hushed voices and whispers of children. They started splitting up to get to me from two sides.

'Oy! Is that you guys or a swarm of cockroaches?' I shouted over my shoulder.

The splattering of feet came to a sudden stop.

'Anna? Tha' ya?' a boy's voice enquired.

'Balls, it's *not* me! I'm on a secret mission! I'm disguised as a *lady*, you juggins!' I tried hard to hold that snort in.

Someone chuckled. I turned around and barked an unladylike laugh.

'You can't walk 'round like that!' Barry said. Abruptly, his concern changed to determination. 'We'll give you protection. Where'd you wanna go?' He walked up to me, showing his missing front teeth and offering a dirty sleeve. 'M'lady?' he said poignantly, trying a manly bow.

I smiled, thanked him, and took the offered aid. The children walked me two blocks to a waiting cab. I curtsied to them for their service to ladyhood and took the hansom to Baker Street.

MRS HUDSON LED me up the stairs and opened the door to Holmes's rooms. Two men were occupying the armchairs. One was Holmes, who started coughing clouds of pipe smoke the moment I entered. The man across from him was moustached and stocky. He wore a wedding band that looked new. Both had their feet on the coffee table as I entered. They seemed comfortable together, good friends. I gathered this was Watson. I took off my hat, stepped closer, and offered him my hand.

'Dr Watson, I presume?'

He nodded and squeezed my fingers lightly. 'Indeed.' He coughed and gazed over my shoulder, as though expecting an additional visitor.

'My name is...' I threw a hasty glance at Holmes, who merely shrugged, '...Anna Kronberg. It is a pleasure to meet you, Dr Watson.' It was difficult to remain calm. He must have expected the male version of me. I could, however, always pretend I had a twin brother.

With a twitch of his arm, Watson offered me his chair.

'Thank you. I was on my feet the whole day.' I sat down. The coffee table would have done, but my dress wouldn't allow such a frivolous seating arrangement.

'My dear Watson, would you give us a moment of privacy?' Holmes asked kindly.

'But of course,' replied Watson, who retreated into the bedroom at once.

'I am truly sorry,' said Holmes quietly. 'My friend was in the area and paid me a surprise visit. I told him that I was expecting you tonight, and he was positively surprised and very much looking forward to meeting you in person. Naturally, I invited him to stay. I couldn't know you would come without your usual disguise.'

'Well, then I'm simply my twin brother's twin sister,' I noted dryly.

He shook his head once. 'If I can make a recommendation, don't lie to him. He will have put two and two together by now. I can promise you that he will not give you away. I would entrust Watson with my life, if necessary.'

Now, I truly felt trapped, and Holmes's reassuring smile only intensified that feeling. 'With how many of your friends did you plan to share my secret, Mr Holmes?'

His eyes narrowed and he replied in the same chilly tone, 'I had not planned to share your secret with anyone. Although, I must admit, it was a mistake to assume you would, for your own sake, maintain the male masquerade and not risk your career out of pure vanity.'

I shot up from my seat. 'Vanity? Mr Holmes, you know *nothing* about me! And stop presuming I wish to discuss my lifestyle with you, or with *anyone* for that matter. I lived quite safely before I met you.'

His gaze softened a fraction. 'You are free to go.'

'You know perfectly well that it is already too late for that.' Huffing, I sank back into the armchair and rubbed my brow. 'Dr Watson will surely be shocked.'

Holmes's mouth twitched.

'Wonderful!' I said, trying to disguise the queasy feeling in my stomach.

At that, Holmes gave a single nod and shouted, 'Watson, you may come back in.'

Watson emerged and Holmes said, 'My dear friend, this is Dr Kronberg.'

The man seemed a little shaken. He nodded, and abruptly sat on the coffee table, as there was only that or the floor to sit upon, and he appeared to need something to support his buttocks momentarily.

'You *really* mean to say...' He was looking at Holmes now. 'You are...' he looked back at me, 'Dr *Anton* Kronberg, from Guy's?' He stared at me, and then back at his friend. 'I went to one of his talks on the works of Dr Snow. I mean, one of... her...her talks.'

'Ah! Watson, my friend.' Holmes leant over and clapped his shoulder. 'Even a man like me has come to accept that there are indeed women with sharp minds. Although quite rare specimens, one cannot help but run into them once or twice.'

Coughing, I held on to my forehead while Watson shot a wild glance at the mantelpiece. Noticing the missing picture, he said sheepishly, 'You took it away. I thought you were fond of her.'

Holmes ignored Watson's remark and I decided to swallow any comments on the matter.

I held the package out to Holmes. 'I wonder whether you can tell me anything about the man who wore these.'

Holmes took the bundle from my hands and laid it on his knees, undid the knot, and opened the paper wrapping. He gazed down at the pile of severed clothes and worn boots, then studied the soles.

'Mr Big Boots,' he noted. 'You dissected him today?'

'I did. He was found by a porter of Guy's, who reported that he heard the whinnying of a horse, the crack of a whip, and gasps of a man he then found just outside the gates. With the help of a colleague, he carried him into my ward. Unfortunately, the man died within minutes. At first, I was unaware that he was Big Boots. I used him as the study subject for a lesson today. We found that he had no entry wound for tetanus and I remembered the man from Hampton, so I checked for restraint marks or needle punctures, but found none. But even if he had been restrained or injected, the marks would have disappeared over the course of a week.'

'But you found something that brought you here, together with the shoes.'

'Yes, I did indeed. If he had eaten an animal with tetanus, he should have had the infection somewhere in his gastrointestinal tract, but there was nothing of the kind. I thought of strychnine next, until I finally found the tetanus infection. Hold on to your armchair, Mr Holmes,' I said. He merely raised an eyebrow. 'It was in his heart.'

'In his heart, you say? How could it have got there?'

'I don't know.' I sighed and rubbed my eyes while uncomfortable thoughts crept into my head.

'What is it?' Holmes enquired, while Watson listened silently and digested the fact that I was not only a female medical doctor, but a well-known one on top of it.

'The man from Hampton hadn't any infection in his gut, either,' I explained quietly. 'Well, aside from cholera. But no tetanus infection. Neither of the two men seemed to have ingested tetanus germs. For the toxins alone to be lethal, one would have to eat quite a lot of diseased animal — the mass of a human — to constitute a lethal dose, I guess.'

'You did not examine the left hemisphere of the Hampton man's brain,' Holmes said. 'Might the source of the infection have been there?'

'Well, I doubt it. It's not entirely impossible, I guess, but...'

'Is there a way to obtain the hemisphere?'

'Cholera fatalities are burned as quickly as possible. The man is ash.'

The man next to me stirred. 'Would someone be so forthcoming as to explain why Dr Kronberg is a woman, and why the two of you are investigating a case where, quite obviously, a crime has not been committed?'

While Holmes explained the case to Watson, my thoughts drifted to what body-snatchers had done decades ago. Anatomical research required bodies for dissections, but medical schools were allowed only the bodies of hanged murderers. These corpses were comparatively rare, and re-used so often that they soon looked more than a little tattered. But where there is demand and money to pay for such services, someone will make an offer. Body-snatchers soon figured out that freshly buried people could be dug up in the dead of the night and sold to medical schools. Very soon after, however, these few cadavers of mostly old or diseased people did not suffice...

Holmes and Watson fell quiet. Their silence interrupted my train of thought. Both were gazing expectantly at me and I wondered whether I had missed a question.

'Watson and I were just discussing the curious incident of the non-existent entry wounds. Watson believes it must be an airborne variety of tetanus.'

'Hmm... That would be a possibility if tetanus germs weren't strictly anaerobic. They peg out when they get a whiff of fresh air.'

Watson coughed. 'Well, then someone must have injected it, but that is impossible!'

'Why do you think so?' asked Holmes.

'Because no one could possibly do such a horrid thing!'

I huffed a laugh. 'How do you think we've learned so much about anatomy in such a short time? History is repeating itself, Dr Watson. Our species has always exploited the weak, be it actively or by ignorance. I was just thinking of the body-snatchers. Surely, you remember the stories? When anatomists wanted *fresh* bodies, it didn't take long for them to get them. How anyone could believe their claim to not have known these were murder victims, is a mystery to me. Several medical doctors even placed orders — pregnant women, children, newborns, and malformed people. And they got them all.'

The thought of the homeless not daring to fall asleep on the streets drove a chill up my spine. The danger was ever present. Someone could suffocate them, and cart them off to the nearest anatomical school.

Watson's shoulders stiffened. Holmes clicked the mouthpiece of his pipe against his front teeth. I continued. 'In a single year, Burke and Hare killed seventeen people in Edinburgh alone and sold all their corpses to Dr Robert Knox, who convinced the authorities that he had no idea they'd been murdered. How can an anatomist not know that he is dissecting a murder victim? After the trial of Burke and Hare, the Anatomical Act was passed. It gave free licence to medical doctors to use donated bodies for dissections. But have you ever wondered who would donate a loved and deceased child, mother, or husband?'

Watson's face paled. He didn't reply, so I answered for him. 'None but the poorest, to feed their children, or themselves. Don't you think the government knew what was going on? Don't you think they turned a blind eye? Don't you think they passed the Anatomical Act to make the butchering of paupers legal? Do you really believe that absolutely *no one* would inject a deadly disease into some crawler or mudlark — a person no one would miss — to test a cure for a disease? One *worthless* life less. Isn't that an acceptable price to pay for the *good of mankind?*'

Watson swallowed, about to reply, but I turned to Holmes and changed the topic. 'What do we do next?'

'We?' he replied, slightly shocked. 'You won't do anything, and I will do some thinking.' With that, he lit his pipe again and leant back in his armchair. After a moment, Watson and I realised that we had been dismissed.

7

A cab dropped me off a short distance from home and I walked the rest of the way — a bit reckless, given my attire. But most people there knew me.

The evening sun threw its last rays over the rooftops, painting the slums in a softer light, making the people look less dirty, sick, and poor. Within the red glow stood a tall and broad-shouldered man with hair like fire — the bright red sticking out every which way. The hint of orange on cheeks and chin was a constant phenomenon, no matter how often he shaved. He grinned at me over everyone's head and I smiled back. Garret O'Hare was a handsome Irishman, warm-hearted and naive in his charming way, with no clue that half the female population of St Giles regularly stared at his buttocks. Well, *and* at the front of his pants.

Like many of my neighbours, he earned his living by stealing whatever valuables he could get his hands on and selling them at the pawnbroker's. But in contrast to most of his colleagues, he was exceptionally good at it. A fact that made me equally proud and anxious.

As did everyone else here, Garret believed I was a young

widow who worked as a medical nurse — lies I had planted to explain my lack of husband and children, and my skills in dealing with infections, stab wounds, fractures, and the like. In return for medical care, my neighbours offered me protection and friendship.

Still smiling, he walked up to me. 'Ain't you pretty!' He came to an abrupt halt and contemplated, his brain visibly rattling. 'You're not been seeing another...bloke?' he enquired, scratching his chin and measuring me from soles to hatband.

I pointed at his shoes. 'You have new boots.'

'Er...yeah. Where've you been?'

'None of your business, Garret. I don't ask you where you *find* all these things, do I?'

'True.' He cleared his throat, contemplated a little longer, then took a step closer and smiled a warm and fuzzy sensation into my chest. The moment I wasn't paying attention to anything but his face, he snatched my hand and gazed at the smallness of it in his large and square paw.

'You can't walk around here looking like that,' he grumbled.

'I surely can. Watch me.' I winked, and took a step away from him. He kept holding on to my hand and followed.

'I'll bring you home,' he decided and walked with me, occasionally throwing a glance of puzzlement at my expensive outfit. He didn't speak another word until we arrived at my doorstep.

'What're you doing tonight?' His voice was thick, and his forget-me-not eyes gleamed like water.

'Hmmm. I might wash,' I answered slowly. 'Undress, most certainly.'

At that, his mouth twitched. He wrapped an arm around my waist and pulled me closer. I hid my smile in his shirt and took a deep breath. He smelled of soap and fresh air.

'And your plans?' I asked through the gap between two

buttonholes. 'Will you be paying a visit to a beautiful lady in a grand villa and unburden her of...this and that?'

'Seems like it,' he said softly and pushed the door to the house open.

'Wait a moment. Did you just pick that lock *and* flirt with me?'

'My pleasure,' he hummed against my neck.

We entered my room and, with his hand resting on the small of my back, he toed the door shut and took a step forward to push me against the wall. Despite his impatience, he was gentle. After all, his weight was about twice mine and he could crush me like an insect. Most certainly that thought had never touched his mind. I'd always wondered how this bulk of a man with shoulders like a bull and sledgehammer fists could possibly work as a burglar. How could he fit through small windows or hide in narrow corners?

My thoughts were cut off by swift fingers unbuttoning my dress. Garret inhaled a sigh when he peeled off the dark silk to reveal my satin corset. His hands searched for the corset's secret openings. I guided him, and heard the wild rumbling of his heart as silk ribbons whispered through eyelets. Rustling of fingers on fabric. The staccato of his breath on my skin. I made short process with his clothes, so much easier to shed than mine. His lips parted when they met mine.

In the glass across the room, the reflection of his broad back reflected the candlelight. Faint lines crisscrossed his skin — marks of the life he led. To me, all about him was gentle and rough at the same time. And every so often, he, with his orange mane and his coarse tongue and paws, made me think of a lion.

'The bed,' he whispered against my mouth.

'Too far away,' I said, and pulled him closer.

He lifted me without effort. His eyes flared as I wrapped my legs around his waist. The soft hairs on his chest tickled my breasts and stomach, and I pressed closer, getting drunk on his warmth and strength. He pushed me up against the wall, shielding me from its chill with his arms, one hand cupping the back of my head, the other my buttocks. And soon I forgot about the complicated web of lies I had woven around myself. In his arms I was but a simple woman, loved by a simple man.

THE CANDLE HAD ALMOST GUTTERED. Its flickering light painted golden sparks onto the curls on Garret's chest. I rolled them around my index finger, lazily, again and again. His ribcage moved up and down — a slow and calming rhythm — and my thoughts began to gallop freely.

I imagined living a normal life. I knew these were idle thoughts. And yet, I needed to think them, as an experiment of *ifs* and *whys* that always lead me back to the path I had taken.

I had chosen a life in disguise because I wanted to practise medicine. I was the only female medical doctor in London. Not officially, though.

What a man had I become! I was so accomplished in speaking, walking, and behaving like a man that no one ever doubted my sex.

I had split my life in two: the male half, which I maintained during the day — Dr Anton Kronberg, renowned bacteriologist — and my female half at night — Anna Kronberg, nurse with an outrageously short haircut. But I lived in the slums where most people made their livings with illegal activities, and so my hacked-off hair didn't really qualify for gossip. My illicit relationship with Garret didn't raise eyebrows, either.

Garret stirred and drew his hand over my back. His face

turned toward me and his breath washed over my face. I kissed him and sat up.

'Isn't it time?' I wondered.

'Huh?'

'Thieving activities. It's almost midnight.'

'Not tonight.' His gaze fell onto my abdomen. His hand followed. He traced the long scar with his fingers and frowned. 'When will you tell me?'

'I can't.' I pushed his hand away and rose to my feet.

'Goddammit,' he groaned. 'You trust me enough to roger you and not break you, but everything else is locked up in that big head of yours!'

'You know more about me than anyone.'

'But you won't even consider marrying me.'

My jaw unhinged. 'Aren't you the hypocrite. Do you suddenly worry about morals, Garret? Really? It is perfectly fine for you to burgle houses and hurt anyone who's between you and the loot, but bedding me without us being husband and wife is wrong?'

He stared at me, not knowing what to say. It had taken him a while to accept that I did not care to be married.

'I never lied to you,' he finally said. 'But you are lying to me. All the time.'

I gazed at him until his eyes lost the brutish glint, then I sat down on the bed. 'Do I really lie to you? I never pretended I could give you more. I told you I wouldn't be able to answer all your questions. You know there are things I cannot share.'

'It's tearing me in half,' he croaked.

I touched his cheek with my fingertips.

'You are my best friend. I give you all I can give. Isn't that enough?'

He shut his eyes, wrapped his fingers around mine, and kissed my palm. 'Not enough.' It was a low growl, one that spoke of pain and hunger. He pulled me closer, wrapped his arms around me, and hoisted me onto him. He pressed his forehead against mine, and sighed. The moment I touched my lips to his, it was as if he ignited. He moulded my body against his own and claimed my mouth.

AN HOUR LATER, the door clicked shut and Garret tiptoed down the creaking stairs. Tense as a bow I sat in my bed, the itch of a wordless peck left on my cheek.

With a groan, I rose, washed my face, and quenched my thirst. I pulled a nightgown over my head and opened the window. Wind sneaked in and played with the curtains. With my tobacco pouch, a bottle of brandy, and a glass as companions, I settled down in my old armchair. Garret would soon be fed up with me, I was certain. Our relationship had always been too undefined for him — it was neither fish nor meat. He often called it *fucking* and that irked me. But why should it?

Yes, why should it?

I wiped the thought away.

The brandy burned its way down my throat, and my mind wandered to Guy's Hospital, where I'd worked from the day I arrived in London. I thought of sweet Mary Higgins, a shy nurse no one seemed to notice. She worked one floor above my ward and had been quietly showing me affection for months. I had believed she would give up soon. Instead, she grew desperate and, without me noticing, followed me down to my basement laboratory one late evening. When I finally heard her approach, it was already too late. She was so close that, when I turned around, all she needed to do was lean in to place a wet kiss on my lips. Startled, I pushed her away, begging her to regain reason. After she left and the initial shock had subsided, I wondered if that kiss could have landed her in gaol, too. Probably not, for she did not know I was a woman. But then, not knowing one is committing a crime is no guarantee that a court will grant leniency.

Living disguised as a man had given me a radically broader view of humanity. *Man*kind! In one disguise or the other, I could observe men and women in their roles and attitudes, and enter either's world of social restrictions and behaviours. Sometimes I felt the insane urge to tell them all to cross-dress. How drastically would the world change then? I laughed at the silly thought.

I had always wondered rather too much, and asked too many questions. Maybe my motive for becoming a scientist was to find reason in all this chaos. After all, I had never felt I belonged to the human race.

I lit a second cigarette and poured another brandy. The night was growing chill. I hugged my knees and gazed up at the ceiling. At the sight of the spots there, Holmes invaded my calm mind. How strange the man was, I thought, and snorted. Was it not I who was the oddity? I was the woman masquerading as a man. I was a scientist and a medical doctor who was occasionally consulted by Scotland Yard. I was trying to solve a crime of which the Yard had no knowledge, and worked on that same case with Sherlock Holmes while fucking an accomplished thief who believed me to be a nurse.

And I owned a cock on straps.

Unusual did not even begin to describe it! I tipped the rest of the brandy into my mouth, flicked the cigarette into the cold fireplace, and wondered onto which shore life would puke me up some day.

8

A few days later, a red-faced Wallace McFadin stormed into my ward, calling my name from afar. I threw up my hands and signalled him to stop making a ruckus. One cannot run and shout in a room full of ill and half-asleep patients.

'My apologies. Me and another student — Farley — we found something,' he said, his voice subdued, then rummaged in his pockets and extracted a small piece of paper.

'You said we should observe everything to find out about the history. The man you dissected a week ago — Farley and I had his right lower arm and hand for today's anatomy lesson. The others got the other parts and I saw his head and torso, so I knew it was him.' McFadin was talking rather fast. 'So, we started dissecting his hand. He still had it balled up into a fist, and then we found this!' He waved a piece of paper in front of my nose. The sweet stink of decomposition combined with creosote was wafting off it. I took it and read. There was only one word written on it in thick, smudged letters:

'Interesting. Thank you, Mr McFadin.'

'Do you think you can find out where he came from, or who he was?'

'I doubt it. I don't even know what the word might mean. Or if it means anything at all.'

McFadin deflated a little. I thanked him once more, went to my office and prepared a wire: *To Mr Sherlock Holmes, 221B Baker Street: Found something. If interested, meet at seven at Carole's, the Strand. A.K.*

I SAT at a small table in the back of Carole's with a candle providing some light. As the time approached twenty past seven, my stomach yowled at me and I decided to order my supper. At that very moment, Holmes walked in, sat down opposite me, and steepled his fingers.

'I know you are fairly busy with much more interesting things than this odd case of mine,' I said. He answered with a frown. 'I expect the criminal world holds countless more intriguing mysteries than this one. However, this might add some spice to the Hampton case, provided you have a clue what it could mean.'

I unfolded the note. He took it gingerly and stared down at it with his eyebrows pushed together.

'A student of mine found it during his anatomy lesson today. He and another student dissected Big Boots's right hand.'

Holmes's face lit up in excitement and he slapped his

palm on the table. Darkness fell. A loud clatter told us that the silverware had jumped off the ledge.

'My apologies.' He struck a match and moved the flame towards the wick. I noticed the contrast of warm light against silver-grey eyes and turned my gaze away.

The waiter appeared, took our orders, and glided away again.

'Mr Holmes?'

'Hmm?'

'Do you know what it could mean?'

Silently, he extracted his magnifying glass, moved closer to the candle, and examined the paper.

'Hmm... No marks. Charcoal, very soft material. No scratch marks. Illegible and smudged...' He straightened up and sat there for a moment, eyes blinking, lips twitching, brow furrowing. I was certain he would have talked to himself had he been alone.

Several long moments passed. The waiter returned and placed our supper on the table. Holmes took no notice of his meal. I had almost finished eating as he seemed to return to the present. 'Do you think we could hear the oriole's call in the Berkshire?'

Hastily, I swallowed the last bit of pork before inhaling it accidentally, opened my mouth, and closed it again with a snap. After a moment of consideration, I answered, 'Broad-moor Lunatic Asylum? I'm sorry, but I can't imagine...' I shook my head. 'The place is enormous and well controlled. You would need to involve a lot of people to hush up a breakout.'

'Yet, the note reads B...OR,' he replied. 'Both men were at Chertsey at a time when one of them was seriously ill and very weak. The distance they travelled could not have been more than twenty miles, I dare say. Within a twenty-mile radius of Chertsey, we have only four places that start with a B: Bracknell, Bagshot, Brookwood, and Broadmoor, and B... OR only fits the latter.'

'What if he was writing down a name?'

'Possible, but not probable if he had any brains. Imagine trying to find Mr Smith, or Mr White, for example. Impossible. Let us assume for now that he knew he was dying and wished to send a message, something that would point the police to the men who infected him with tetanus, given he had indeed been infected, which is likely, if not certain. If the two men were in Broadmoor and broke out, without anyone alerting the Yard, then we have an intriguing situation and one must wonder why it was not reported. But I am getting ahead of myself.'

Holmes was all focus and excitement. He may have appeared calm and even rigid to the onlooker, but the movements of his entire body were many, very quick and small — eyes narrowing a fraction and opening up again, lips compressing, corners of his mouth pulling up and down very slightly, fingers tapping on the tabletop, breath slowing and speeding up, feet shuffling ever so slightly. He vibrated.

'It appears that both were victims of medical malpractice, to say the least,' he went on. 'I believe it is time to pay a visit to Broadmoor Lunatic Asylum together with my old acquaintance, Inspector Lestrade.' He leant back, looking expectantly at me.

'When?'

'Tomorrow morning.'

'I'm sorry, but I have to be at the hospital. Besides, you don't need me there and I'd rather not meet with the police more often than absolutely necessary. But I'm very much interested in the outcome, of course. Shall we meet after the raid?'

'So it is a raid now.'

'Sounds more exciting than a mere visit.' I pulled a corner of my mouth up.

'Very well! We will meet at my quarters at eight. Mrs Hudson will provide us with supper.'

9

At eight o'clock sharp, I knocked on the dark oak door. Mrs Hudson answered with a cautious look on her face. Violin music poured down the staircase and I was surprised by the aggressiveness of Holmes's play. Climbing the seventeen steps, I tried to recall and avoid the ones that produced a shy squeal when stepped upon. I settled at the topmost stair and leant my head against the door. With eyes shut and ears wide open, I listened to *La Tempesta di Mare*, my favourite of Vivaldi's works. Holmes put such force into his play that my heart fidgeted like a salmon on a riverbank.

He finished the piece and I rose to my feet, about to knock, when he started the *Presto*. My hand hovering over the doorknob. I dared not move a muscle. There was a reason I stayed away from music halls. I would sit in my chair and cry my heart out.

The violin fell quiet again and I heard Holmes say, 'When would you think it appropriate to enter?'

Slowly my hand lowered itself onto the knob, turned it automatically, and opened the door. Just before the fully open door would reveal my face, I rubbed the moisture off my cheeks.

'Thank you, that was...enjoyable,' I croaked, wondering how the deuce he had noticed my presence.

'It got a bit laborious toward the end, I must say.' Holmes's flushed face wore a wild expression. He stared at the bow that was just as ruffled as he, and made an irritated flicking movement that sent loose strands of horse hair flying.

'I loved it!' I said, cleared my throat, and looked away. 'The raid was a disaster?'

'There's nothing of interest at Broadmoor,' he said, setting violin and bow on the desk, or, rather, on top of all the papers. Then he fetched a Persian slipper that he happened to be using as a tobacco pouch. In a different situation, I would have laughed. Now I could only frown. He stuffed and lit his pipe and settled down to smoke.

'So what now?' I enquired.

'Nothing. I dropped the case,' he replied, producing a cloud of blue smoke with each word.

I watched him for a moment and could not believe his words. He was angry, not bored or disappointed. 'Tell me, Mr Holmes, did you play Vivaldi because you did not know how to produce the lie so that I would believe it? Or because you have a problem lying to me? Forget the last; it was a stupid assumption.'

Slowly he tore his gaze off the ceiling and glued it to my face. 'That is a strong accusation.'

'Am I mistaken?'

'Certainly!'

'Be careful, Mr Holmes, I may end up throwing one of your possessions out of the window.' My jest didn't have the desired effect. All he did was narrow his eyes and lean forward.

'I believe it is time to leave now, Miss Kronberg.'

I noticed the omission of my title. Anger tickled my insides. 'I think it is time to go to Broadmoor, *Sherlock*.'

His expression grew icy. 'Do what you see fit.' He lent back and recommenced staring at the ceiling.

'I always do. See you in the Berkshire.' I opened the door a crack. He leapt off his armchair, shot his long arm out, and slammed the door shut. I was trapped inside.

'You are hindering my investigation and I must insist you leave Broadmoor to me.' It was as though he had opened another door to let me see the danger lurking behind his calm facade. I had just poked a stick into the jaguar's cage.

'How do I hinder your investigation? So far, I have helped bring it forward.'

'You haven't. Any suggestion, clue, or deduction you made, I had already made. I let you believe your suggestions were useful.'

'Why would you do that?'

'It amused me,' he said coldly.

My fingertips began to tingle. 'And now you are tired of the clown?'

'Quite so.' He didn't move.

'Should I scream for the police?' I said, bored.

'Please do that. I may reveal interesting details about you.'

'I don't believe a word you say.'

He twitched a shoulder as though he couldn't be bothered to carry out a proper shrug. Unmoving, he gazed down at me, superiority seeping from every pore.

'Isn't it curious,' I said softly, gazing up into his face. There were only inches between us now. 'How the need to wear armour only reveals the tender spots.' I dipped my fingertips into his shirt — there, where the heartbeat was.

His gaze flickered, his hand released the door, and I slipped away.

I BOUGHT A BAKED POTATO, ate it, and paid a visit to Garret to borrow a rope. He seemed rather puzzled when I told him I needed it to climb a tree. Once home, I packed a few provisions, a blanket, a pair of trousers, and was off to catch the last train to Crowthorne.

Close to midnight, the train arrived at Crowthorne Station. I spotted Holmes. His presence didn't surprise me. He kept his distance and neither of us acknowledged the other. Clouds covered the dark sky. A perfect night to burgle an asylum.

It took me fifteen minutes to reach the edge of the pitch black forest. I slipped into a woods, took cover behind a large tree, pulled off my boots, and changed into the pair of trousers. Soft footfalls announced Holmes. Quickly, I stuffed shoes and skirts into my rucksack and strapped it tightly onto my back. Any noise coming from things moving within it had to be avoided.

Holmes was behind me, and dangerously close. He could probably have touched my shoulder had he stretched out his hand.

I ducked and ran. Behind me, I heard him huff a quiet growl. I had finally rattled his composure.

I wasn't too worried about him catching up with me. I had spent my childhood in the large forest surrounding my village. Climbing slick trees was not a great challenge, and I enjoyed the silent run through the woods. Holmes was only a city dweller and hadn't a chance against me.

After roughly half a mile, the canopy lightened and the intimidating outer wall of Broadmoor Lunatic Asylum looked down upon me. I ran along it and found a tree that suited my purpose — a mighty oak, split in two by lightning. One half of the tree was still alive, with a thick branch that reached over the wall.

I climbed up and nestled close to its trunk, my legs hugging the branch. The asylum stretched below me. A few lit windows dotted the larger buildings; the occasional outside lamp spit light onto the grass. Broadmoor almost looked like a small city, asleep and quiet. During my first two years at Guy's, the annual hygiene inspection of a number of asylums had been one of my tasks. Among them had been Broadmoor, and this circumstance served me well now.

To the left I saw the main building that Holmes must have visited earlier that morning. It was the oldest, and now served as the lowest-security block. It housed harmless cases such as female petty thieves with depression or a nervous tic. Farther to the right were the five male blocks built a year after the first. Most of these inhabitants were harmless as well.

And then, far to the right, were the two high security blocks — one for women and one for men. Many of these inmates were insane murderers, who lived in isolation and got their daily ration of groats pushed through a hatch at the bottom of a heavy iron door. Well away from me, the tall chimney of the central heating facility poked into the night sky, much like a warning index finger. I wondered whether this building might serve as a hiding place during summer months.

After a moment of consideration, I decided to first investigate the high security blocks that lay at some distance from the remaining complex, and thus the most suited to any secret undertaking. Hopefully, I could collect information without running into the security men, who were armed with club and revolver.

A quiet snap sounded nearby. I peered down and spotted the slender silhouette of a man. He moved easily in the dark, peering at the ground as though trying to find my footprints. Could he see anything on the ground in this darkness? And even if his night vision were excellent, the soil was comparatively dry and the layer of leaves covering the forest floor was thick. I held my breath and waited for him to stop and bend down, to find traces of my presence. But he kept walking without so much as a swift stoop, passed my oak, and disappeared behind a bend of the wall.

I waited a few moments to make sure he wouldn't come back, then slung my knapsack off, and strapped it to the tree. Carrying a length of rope over my shoulder, I balanced along the branch. Just beyond the fifteen-foot-high wall, I tied the rope to the branch and climbed down. The inner wall reached an elevation of only six feet and wouldn't be too hard to scale.

I rubbed dirt onto my too white face, and started running. With a leap, I caught the top of the shorter wall and pulled myself up. Patches of silvery light began moving across the lawn. I gazed up at the sky. The cloud cover had opened to reveal a sickle of moon.

Painfully aware of my sudden visibility, I dropped down on the other side of the wall. The resulting thud sounded too loud in my ears. A bush provided limited cover and I used it to take a look around. Not a soul in sight. I waited, ears and eyes sharp, but Broadmoor Lunatic Asylum was deadly quiet. I wondered what Holmes was doing. Or, for that matter, what I was doing — a woman disguised as a man, pretending to be accomplished at breaking into criminal asylums.

I swallowed the snort that wanted to rip through my nervousness, and almost jumped at the hooting of a tawny owl. Pressing my fist against my chest, I took a few slow breaths to calm my heart and then ran to the next hiding place — a small tool shed close to the high security block for men. Cautiously, I sneaked up to the building. There was a window low enough for me to reach. I peered inside, expecting to see a cell. The last time I'd visited, the block had consisted of parallel rows of cells along a narrow corridor. There was no need for a hall for socialising, because allowing these men to mix would have resulted in violence, perhaps even a mass breakout.

From what I was seeing, this block had been rebuilt substantially. Several of the cells had a wall or two taken out — at least partially — and had been merged into a long hall. There was no one to be seen, but a large number of small bunks sent shivers up my spine: each was equipped with four fetters — two for the ankles, two for the wrists. The room looked tidy, as though recently cleaned up.

With a wildly thumping heart, I turned away and started towards the female block when I came across fresh wheel tracks in the grass. The cart must have been fully laden, for the tracks were deep despite the dryness of the soil. I followed them. My stomach roiled with foreboding. I turned a corner and the heating facility came into view. Its heavy iron door stood ajar. A glow of fire licked the trodden lawn.

Inching closer, I took each bit of cover I could find. Voices inside the building reverberated on the thick stone walls and trickled through the dark. One of them I recognised as the rasp of Nicholson — Broadmoor's superintendent. But no matter how I strained my ears, I could not understand what was being said.

I had come so close that I could peer through the door into a room with a large oven. One man was talking — Nicholson — while another shovelled coal, and two others hurled one large sack after another into the fire. The effort it took and the sharp downward bend in the middle of each sack identified their contents. Strangely, my mind swallowed the information without stirring up the slightest trace of emotion. Only after the sweet smoke had crawled from the chimney into my nostrils did horror shake my limbs.

Gasping, I pressed my face into my sleeve and hugged my knees tightly, trying to resist the urge to run inside and rip Nicholson's eyes out. It took me a while to collect myself. There was nothing to be done, so I decided to leave. Breathing was almost impossible with that large lump in my throat. I raced from cover to cover, and scrambled to scale the inner wall. I found my oak and the rope dangling from it, and made my way up. Once safe, I lay flat on the thick branch and wept.

'I'd have preferred you stayed in London,' a quiet voice said.

My head snapped up and I stared at Holmes, who sat on the very same branch, leaning his back against the trunk.

'Leave me alone.' I choked out the words and rose to my feet.

He didn't move.

I undid the rope and pushed past him.

'Wait,' he said.

I couldn't bear his company now. Or any company, for that matter. I slung my rucksack on my back and slid down the tree. He exclaimed quietly while making his way down, too. Before Holmes's shoes even touched the forest floor, I was gone.

I did my best to race my lungs out of my chest. It did nothing to calm me. The trees grew less dense, and I stumbled into a small clearing. In its centre, moonlight reflected off a pond — a circular, black silk surface, its rims decorated with clumps of grass, fenberry shrubs, and pale green sphagnum moss. It was commonly believed that the moor meant a slow and silent death — just another of the foolish sentiments of our species. To me, the moor meant beauty and peace, because few would dare enter. And a man like Holmes would certainly avoid it. My decision was made.

Slowly, I approached the small lake. With every step I

took, the moss wobbled and swung, the oscillations reaching as far as ten feet in each direction. I placed my bare feet with care, and mostly on thick grass clumps where they were within reach. At the edge of the water I dropped my knapsack, and shed trousers and shirt. Now only in my underclothing, I took one more step, sat down, and slid my legs into the lake. The turf sank down, softly releasing me into the water. My outstretched toes did not reach the mud. The lake was deep enough for me to dive. And I did.

Blackness engulfed me, and I let the cold water wash off the stench and the images of corpses in bags thrown carelessly into the roaring fire of Broadmoor's enormous oven. My lungs began to protest, my ribcage contracted, eager to suck in the fresh air and expel what I had used up. I kept diving and, just before darkness was about to swallow my mind, I pushed my head through the lake's surface. With a long sigh, I greeted the crisp night air of the Berkshire forest.

A movement at the lake's edge caught my eye. Someone was hastily undressing, then stopped as I peered in his direction. I made a mental note not to underestimate his abilities again. He seemed unsure how to walk onto the swimming plant cover, and I wondered how he was planning to rescue me.

After he'd pulled his trousers back up, I swam to my pile of clothes. Holmes retreated a few steps.

'What the dickens are *you* doing here? I thought we agreed that I have nothing to add to this investigation?' I hissed.

'Well, why then do you keep intruding upon it?' he replied coldly. 'And what is this anyway?' He flicked his arm in my direction. 'An attempt to drown yourself because this case overwhelms your sensibilities? Or do you simply try to attract my attention?'

'You are... You...' I pointed a stiff index finger at him, but words failed me.

He crossed his arms over his chest.

'You mosquito buggering fopdoodle!' burst from my mouth.

'Get dressed,' he said, and disappeared into the woods.

Seething, I pulled myself out of the pond, wrung water from my sopping underclothes, and put my trousers and shirt back on.

I found Holmes — or rather the glint of his cigarette — about a hundred yards away from the bog. He leant on a tree, hands in his pocket, his smoke dangling from the corner of his mouth. Unspeaking, we walked in the direction of the train station until we found a dry place to sit. I extracted the little food and drink I had from the depths of my knapsack, and placed it between us.

'I am tired of your attempts at manipulating me. And I'm so tired of your arrogance,' I said. 'But I'm here now and I won't go away. Accustom yourself to it.'

He stared into the dark, and spoke quietly. 'Last winter, I investigated a burglary and paid a group of street urchins to tail the suspect. The man was killed. One of the boys saw the murderer. Two days later, the boy was found clubbed to death. He was eleven years old. His murderers wished to send me a warning, so they spread the boy's intestines along the riverbank.'

He fell silent, and gradually I understood his reluctance to involve me in this investigation. I understood it, and respected it, but I wouldn't accept it. Was his reluctance based solely on the death of the boy? Had I been wrong in believing he thought himself superior, not needing the help of anyone else, let alone a woman? Perhaps it was silly of me to maintain this preconception that all men expected women to be the lesser sex. I wiped prejudice away for a moment and gazed up at him.

'I'll never again put anyone in danger for the sake of a case,' he said finally. 'Anyone but myself, of course.'

I opened the small bottle of brandy I'd brought, filled my one cup, and handed it to him. He took it with a nod.

'I am sorry,' I said softly, 'for you and the boy.'

Slowly, the crickets' music faded. It was obviously time for them to go to bed. I, however, was wide awake.

'You think you should have known better,' I continued. 'You do think that rather often.' It wasn't meant to be a question. I turned toward him and touched his elbow. 'Absolutely nothing can be learned from another's cruelty.'

He looked at me, quizzical at first, but after a moment, his eyes grew cold and hard.

'My apologies. It was not my intention to humiliate you.'

'You didn't. A memory did,' he replied and turned away.

And then I knew that my assumption had been correct: Someone had torn him apart a long time ago. No one is born untrusting, only made so. I refilled the cup he held in his hand. He nodded and took a mouthful, then offered it to me. I tipped its entire contents into my mouth. We were quiet for a long time, eating, drinking, and contemplating, until I interrupted the silence. 'The flame was white.'

'Yes, I know.'

There was no use in calling the police. A white flame burns so hot that bones and even teeth are turned to ash within twenty minutes.

'What else did you see?' I asked.

'Much as what you saw.'

'You are an exceptional detective and I can understand that you believe I'm in your way.'

He huffed with amusement.

'But I won't budge,' I continued. 'I have a personal

interest in this crime. They are experimenting with highly dangerous bacteria and they shouldn't be able to get past London's best bacteriologist.'

Groaning, he rubbed his brow. 'Dare I ask what your plan might be?'

'I venture you wouldn't be able not to ask. Both victims were infected with tetanus, one of them with cholera, as well. From now on, I will focus my research on tetanus and become such an attractive target that whoever is behind this will pay me a visit. There must be a number of medical doctors involved, and one of them will want my knowledge and services sooner or later.'

Holmes exhaled audibly, but, after a while, he said, 'That seems sensible.'

It took me a moment to digest that.

Then he added, 'All evidence is destroyed, all victims burned. It will take them a while to start anew, but that probably suits them well. They'll have to keep their heads low for a few weeks. They have to select new test subjects, and that can be done in quiet. I'm quite certain they find their victims in workhouses.' His smug smile told me he had a plan, too.

'How do you plan to get into the workhouses? Not as a pauper?'

'Isn't that the obvious strategy?' He seemed a little disappointed by my question.

'It is. I am just having problems picturing you in rags.'

He twitched his eyebrows at me, then struck a match and looked at his watch. It was two o'clock and the night had gone chilly. Somewhere close by, the tawny owl hooted again. I unfolded my blanket, moved closer to him, and draped it over his legs and mine.

'What happened in Broadmoor this morning?' I enquired.

A hiss through his teeth. 'Nicholson was warned and had

the whole of the night to clean up. It was as clear as the bright daylight, but Lestrade didn't notice it, as usual.'

Images of Nicholson supervising the burning of corpses crept back into my mind. I shuddered. 'Who warned Nicholson?'

'Gibson.'

'What?'

'He must have been in an exceptionally smart mood and wired the local police force, asking for reinforcements for the raid the following morning. As he did this against my instructions, he didn't dare inform us before we left. The constable who received the wire is Nicholson's nephew. Naturally, he warned his uncle.'

'Balls! I mean...sorry! *Drat* is what I meant. My apologies, sometimes I'm a bucket.'

'A what?'

'Bucket,' I said, tapping my skull with my index finger. *'Empty vessel.'*

He slapped his knees and gave a bark of a laugh, then muffled himself face down in his sleeve. I noticed that this was only the second time I had seen him laughing.

After a long moment, he said, 'I believe your vessel is full to the brim.'

Abashed, I fell silent.

'Although at times you are a muckspout,' he added.

10

O n September 10th, an unidentified female torso was discovered under a railway arch in Pinchin Street. No other body parts were found in the vicinity. The papers were full of it and all of London suspected Jack the Ripper; only Holmes did not. Again, bobbies were swarming Whitechapel and all the other slums of London, making it exceedingly difficult for me to change from Anna into Anton, and back again.

Over the previous weeks, Holmes had spent considerable time disguised as a pauper, but had refocused his energies on the torso case. Our two dead men were still unidentified. But I had other things demanding my attention as well.

The government had awarded me a substantial grant for the isolation of tetanus germs. A visit to Robert Koch's laboratory in Berlin was included in the funding. In two weeks' time, I would leave London for the whole of three months. The prospect of seeing my father made me feel rather fluttery in my chest.

Despite the exciting news, my stomach wouldn't stop aching. I was certain that word of my tetanus research had spread, and that the men behind the Broadmoor experiments had their eyes on me already.

~

I WAS at home when an urgent knock interrupted my kitchen scrubbing.

'Yes?' I called, and the door creaked open. Barry stood in the door frame, a small boy of ten years, face pale beneath the grime, his hands shaking. The whole child was a picture of agitation.

'What is it?' I said, dropping the rag in the bucket.

'My mum,' he croaked, 'is very sick.'

I snatched my doctor's bag and we were both out of the house in less than a minute.

He lived just around the corner in a two-storey house, which mould had taken hostage many years ago. The privy was always overflowing, for it had to accommodate thirty or so inhabitants, all in various stages of dire poverty. Without a single window or door intact, the house and whoever lived inside were at the weather's mercy all year round. Here in St Giles, it was a house like many others.

We climbed the crooked stairs to the second floor. It was dark and I stumbled several times. The missing windowpanes had been replaced with mildewed cardboard and potato sacks filled with rubbish. Milky-white daylight fingered through the shadows and painted the decline in harsh colours.

We passed through a narrow corridor and entered a room that smelled like fermenting excrement. I stopped in the door frame and squinted, waiting for my eyes to adapt to the poor light. The heaps on the floor were children. They lifted their heads and greeted me with weak smiles, showing a wreckage of yellowed and blackened teeth. In the corner lay a straw mattress that seemed to have been clubbed to death.

Should I have earned a thousand pounds each month, it wouldn't have been enough to turn life in St Giles to something acceptable. Several thousand people lived there under the worst conditions. Women gave birth on filthy stairways or down in the streets. Their newborns had a survival rate of thirty per cent, at most. Of those, only another thirty per cent made it to adulthood, only to die of violence, disease, or undernourishment.

Barry and I approached the static pile on the mattress.

'Mum? She's here,' whispered the boy.

The blanket moved and a pair of blue eyes peered up into mine, losing focus soon thereafter.

'Sally, what happened?' I asked.

She mumbled something unintelligible.

I touched her forehead — it was scorching hot — then pulled the blanket down to her waist and unbuttoned her dress to palpate her abdomen. Both spleen and liver were enlarged, and she groaned as I pressed my fingers into the soft flesh. I took a candle from my bag, lit it, and moved the light closer to her. There were rose-coloured patches on her lower chest.

'Barry, does she talk funny sometimes?'

'Yes, ma'am.'

He had never called me *ma'am* before. Startled, I turned towards him. 'Barry, your mum has typhoid fever. Do you know what that is?'

He nodded, his eyes wide in shock.

I looked around in the room. There was a hole in the wall which must have been a functional fireplace once. The thought of the approaching winter and my imminent journey to the continent left an astringent taste of urgency in my mouth.

They couldn't even make a fire there to at least warm the winter up a little. The biting cold would penetrate the missing windows and doors and the rotten walls to turn anyone who wasn't up to it into a frozen corpse. And no matter how loud one begged, the winter would not retreat until five months later.

I turned back to the boy. 'Barry, I'm leaving for the continent in a few days. You must be her nurse. I will teach you how. We will move her into my quarters tomorrow, and you will take care of her there. Do you think you can do that?'

His eyes lit up and he nodded again, this time vigorously.

The following day, we carried Sally to my flat. A swarm of children helped to convey the makeshift bunk on which she lay. I had set up a sleeping corner with clean blankets, several jugs of fresh water, and a bed pan. There was nothing else we could do but give her a dry, clean, and warm place. I left the boy with money for wood, coal, and food and instructed him where to get clean water. He would sleep there with his mother until she either felt healthy enough to return to her own home, or until I arrived back at the end of December.

I desperately hoped my rooms would not be invaded by the other thirty inhabitants of Barry's house.

11

My journey to the continent began on September 30th.
On the ship to Hamburg, I read Watson's *A Study in
Scarlet*. The whole of London seemed to know Sherlock
Holmes, and I had the feeling this educational gap needed to
be filled. When I read about Holmes flogging corpses in the
morgue my barks of laughter drew the ire of my fellow
passengers. I tried to stifle my enthusiasm then, but had to
admit that Mr Holmes certainly had all his buttons on when
it came to detecting.

And when I read about Holmes trying to explain his
newly developed haemoglobin test to Watson, and Watson
failing to grasp its significance for solving murders and appre-
hending the culprits, I grew sober. Holmes's childlike enthusiasm over a new discovery, his capacity for highly advanced
thinking, and his being the only one who understood the
consequences of scientific progress felt all too familiar to me.

Some of Watson's descriptions gave a weak glimpse of
Holmes as I knew him. Some were very precise indeed, while
others seemed to speak of a stranger. But doesn't each friend
provide a different angle on our character? Wouldn't one be

extraordinarily lucky to find a friend who is able to see the whole picture and still respect all of it?

At times, Watson's narrative annoyed me a little. He described symptoms of poisoning but did not draw obvious conclusions. His attention seemed focussed on the superficial only. He would think it noteworthy how people were dressed, the colour of their eyes, or the condition of the wallpaper at the crime scene. He saw and described, but never made the connections. I had to pull myself together and not slap the journal to my forehead. How could two so very different men possibly be friends? Perhaps because Holmes was, in a way, the least judgemental person I had ever met. He could easily accept Watson's blindness. In that, of course, Watson did not differ from the ninety-nine per cent of mankind.

But one thing made Watson very special indeed: he did not resent Holmes's arrogance, which was the main reason the majority of people avoided him. Holmes made people feel small. I wondered whether Watson sometimes did feel insignificant next to Holmes, and had accepted it as a small price to pay for his friendship. Somewhere inside my strange heart, I felt respect growing for the stocky surgeon.

A TRAIN TOOK me from Hamburg to Berlin. The city came into view and I began to vibrate. Here, I had defended my thesis. That had been an exception: Although my medical studies had taken place at the Leipzig University, I'd had spent several months at Berlin's Charité Hospital and had met Robert Koch. He was part of my thesis committee, and for his convenience, my PhD defence was relocated to Berlin.

And it was in Berlin that I'd had lost my so-called innocence. But it wouldn't help to pull the old horrors out of the pirate's chest again.

A student of Dr von Behring picked me up from the train station and showed me to my quarters. There was a small eating house close by where I took a late supper. It was so odd to hear everyone speaking German. It did not feel like my language anymore, sounding so clipped and rough.

After I had eaten, I made my way back to my temporary room and quickly fell asleep, exhausted from my long journey.

The following morning, I took the tram to the Charité. Although I was familiar with the place and still knew some of the staff there, a feeling of my own insufficiency and insignificance hit hard. Koch's laboratory was the most modern and best equipped I had ever seen. I got a friendly reception from both Dr von Behring, a specialist in diphtheria, and Dr Kitasato, and expert in tetanus. A lab space was assigned to me, as well as equipment for my personal use and an assistant to share with Dr Kitasato. The two of us aimed to isolate tetanus germs as a first step in the production of a vaccine.

We used solid media to isolate the germs, a novelty advanced by Dr Koch. I was surprised at how much easier the cultivation of pure bacterial cultures was compared to using traditional liquid media. We decided I would focus on the isolation of the germ itself and Dr Kitasato would spend his energies on the characterisation of the tetanus toxin that we suspected caused the typical muscle spasms. With these complementary approaches, we hoped to shorten the long and winding path to vaccine development.

For two months, we worked nearly around the clock. Twice I woke up face down on my lab bench, but more often I found myself close to falling off my stool. During that intense time, all bodily needs were a nuisance. Eating and sleeping felt like a waste of time. Most nights, I forgot to change into my female self. But despite all my efforts, I had no success in cultivating tetanus bacteria. Before the dawn of my third month in Berlin, I decided to leave everything behind and pay a visit to my father.

ON THE TRAIN TO LEIPZIG, I saw my childhood rushing past, interwoven with the familiar countryside. It made my heart ache in a good way. My father was waiting at the station, holding on to one of his coat buttons — twisting and turning it — and waiting for his only child.

I pushed through the crowd, anxiously wondering whether he still loved me. What a silly thought, I realised, when I flung my arms around him, pressing my face to his warm chest and inhaling scents of fresh wood shavings. He held me tight as though he hadn't seen me for years. I pushed a quiet sob into his coat as I realised we had indeed not seen each other for a very long time.

He released me then and gazed into my face, slightly abashed. We rarely hugged. Besides, his daughter looked like a man.

We left the station, climbed onto his cart, and he flicked the whip across the backs of his two yellow Haflinger ponies. He asked me about my work in Berlin and about the journey. We both felt a little awkward, as though we had to get to know each other again.

When we reached the forest around Naunhof, I asked my father to stop for a moment so I could change into my women's clothing. Upon my return from the woods, I pointed at the horses. 'Don't you think these two old ladies should retire?'

He only grunted in response and I got the feeling that something was worrying him. With my hand on his knee, I said, 'Anton? Can I ask you something and you promise me not to be mad?'

Another grunt — he probably guessed what was coming.

'You did get the money I sent you every month?'

He nodded, but did not look at me.

'Are you using it? At all?'

He shook his head, finally turning his face towards me, wearing an apologetic frown.

'Why?' I asked, unbelieving. 'I mean... Sorry, it's your own business. You can do with it what you want, of course, but please tell me if I offended you by sending you money. Er... Did I offend you?' I stammered.

He snorted and shook his head. 'Anna, you behave like the elephant in the china store who's finally learned that she has pretty big bum.'

'What?'

'Never mind. I put the money aside. And before you ask why, I did it because I know that one day it will all come out and you'll have to hide somewhere. I saved all the money you sent. You will have it back when you need it.'

For a long moment I was speechless.

'You always tell me I get the brains from Mother, but I don't think that's true. You are quite a brainy carpenter.'

He blushed a little, and we both fell silent again.

An hour later, we crossed the river Mulde at the Pöppelmann Bridge. I was about to see my old home again and the thought sped up my heart and lungs. Then I remembered the money. 'Papa, I have to tell you something.'

He gazed at me with one bushy eyebrow pulled up. Every time he did that, he looked like a ten-years-younger and very smug version of himself. I had to hold on to myself so as not to kiss his brow.

'I sent you only half of my savings. The other half is in the bank. Goes there every month. I know that I may need a safe hiding place and some money to get me through several months.'

Now his other eyebrow went up, too.

'Last year I bought a small cottage in the countryside. It's in an awful state, but when I need it, I'll fix it up. I have a safe place. So would you *please* use the money I gave you?'

He patted my knee and huffed.

'Aw! Come now, old carpenter!' I poked his ribs with my elbow. 'Allow the ladies their much deserved retirement, and don't turn them into salami. And get yourself two new ponies!'

He wrapped an arm around me, and the two horses pulled us up the hill. We turned a corner and I could see it — the small stone house with the mossy straw roof that was now dusted with snow. Everything looked as it had when I left — the garden, the hen house, the wood shed, and the carpenter's workshop. I spotted the large cherry tree that had borne my weight over years, and felt the familiar pang in my chest that always came with the memory of the place I'd called home for the best part of my life. Coming home made me feel calm and nervous at the same time.

We were both hungry, so I cooked dinner and we drank the brandy I had brought from London. He sat in his armchair and I on the rug in front of him, both of us close to the fireplace with the heat toasting our feet. And very soon thereafter I fell asleep.

I woke up with the winter sun shining through the window of my old bedroom, which was really more a cupboard than anything else. Surprised, I noticed that my father kept it exactly as I'd left it.

I got up, washed, dressed, and walked into the small sitting room. Familiar scents, and the furniture I'd climbed when I was little, greeted me like long-forgotten friends.

Quietly I said hello to the tattered armchair, hoping that no one would hear me talking to it or see me stroking its bleached backrest.

I spotted our two wooden chairs, nicked and gouged as long as I could remember, and the small table where we used to sit and eat. Then I noticed the doily. I walked over to inspect. Someone had a good hand at bobbin lace. The room was tidier than I remembered it, in its best days. There was but one explanation — female influence.

The scraping noise coming from the workshop lured me outside, and I found my father cutting fine carvings into a wardrobe door. I leant against the shed and watched him. His skill had always fascinated me. He had the rare ability to look at an apparatus, a tool, or a building and know instantly how it worked and how it was constructed. He could fix machines he had never set eyes upon before. He would open them carefully, poke and wiggle at their intestines with his small clasp-knife, and then, with utmost concentration, he would scrunch up his face and figure out everything in minutes. He could do that with people, too. After a moment of scrutinising a stranger, he knew what character was hidden inside. Or he would look at me and know what I felt. It was very annoying.

He noticed my presence and smiled.

'Who is the woman? Do I know her?' I had to attack before he did.

'Katherina.' He didn't look up from his work.

'Oh, really? I like her.' She had been living on our street since I was little and had been like an aunt to me. I started wondering when they had fallen in love, and whether he would ask her to marry him. Ah, what a silly thought. Of course he would ask her. Most likely he already had done so.

'I'm happy for you,' I said, and my father's cheeks reddened. He answered with a grunt.

'Breakfast?' I offered, shivering and eager to get back inside.

He slapped his stomach once. 'Had mine two hours ago, but there's some space left.' He tried his evil grin and mocked me, 'Off with you to the kitchen, woman!'

'For your information, I do know some self-defence,' I lied, my arms akimbo.

'Shall I ask our maid, Dr Kronberg?' he retorted.

'You could surely afford one with all that money you hide under your mattress.' I knocked the wood shavings off his shoulders.

We kicked the slushy snow off our shoes, took them off, and walked into the warm kitchen. Leaning against the counter, we drank strong coffee and ate porridge, scorching our tongues and gullets.

'Are you happy, Anna?'

This question did not come unexpected, but I was still grateful for the food in my mouth, for it gave me a moment to think before answering, 'Mostly, yes.'

He wanted to add something, but only scratched an ear.

'What is it?'

'Hmm... I'm getting old,' he mumbled.

'We all are. But what is bothering you?'

'When parents begin to grow older, they think about...grandchildren.'

I gazed up into his face as my heart skidded along. He didn't know what had happened eight years before, and I would never dare tell him. I knew it would hurt him badly and he would want to avenge his daughter.

I swallowed.

'Do you have someone, Anna?'

I thought of Garret then, and although I tried to hide that silly smile, my father caught my expression. He looked satisfied. For a moment, at least.

'Who is he?' he asked, pretending casualness and stirring his porridge. Then he paused and added carefully, 'Or, she?'

I laughed. 'The man's name is Garret. He is Irish and the best thief in the neighbourhood.'

The porridge flew from my father's mouth and sailed in little flecks down onto the floor. He coughed. 'A thief!'

'You know that I live in the slums. Most people there have no options.'

His face grew red with anger.

'Garret is kind. If you two met, you'd get along splendidly. And...he loves me.'

'Do you love him?'

I dropped my gaze. 'It's of no consequence. He wouldn't be able to accept my...style of living.'

'You won't know that if you don't tell him.'

I placed my empty bowl in the kitchen sink, and picked up an ewer of water, and began washing the dishes. 'I can't.'

'It's actually quite easy. You knock on his door, step into his room... He does have a place, doesn't he? Oh, good. And then you say, "Garret, I wear men's clothes most of the time. What do you think about that?"'

Slowly, I turned and blinked at my father. He pinched his lips together, but soon the laughter jumped out of him and rocked his belly.

'Well, that would be one way of doing it,' I mused.

He grew sober, and said, 'I know you are afraid. But do you really want to be alone? Have no one to talk to? I spent years alone and don't wish that on anyone, least of all you.' He reached out and cupped my cheek.

I dashed a tear away. 'I will think on it.'

He nodded. I watched him shuffle about in the kitchen, and felt a sudden urge to throw my arms around him and not let go for a very long time. But, of course, I did no such thing.

'Anton?'

'Hmm?'

'You are the best Father in the world.'

His head snapped up, his face reddened and he hastily turned away.

I continued, 'We always talk eye to eye, and I'm so grateful you allow this. I'm so grateful that you treat your child with respect and love. Like an equal.'

He looked into my eyes then, his brow in crinkles, but he didn't speak. I had taken his words away.

At last I said, 'I don't think I will ever marry. No one would tolerate a woman like me. No one who is quite right in his mind.'

'Why would you say that?'

'Look at me, Father,' I said gently. 'Have you ever seen a woman like me? A woman who looks like a man, behaves like a man, can't ever keep her mouth shut, and works in an exclusively male domain? I actually *did* consider marrying a woman so that all my male colleagues would stop whispering behind my back and the nurses would stop flirting with me!'

'Don't talk about yourself like that!'

'But it is true,' I said softly.

My father stood there helpless and silent, with his arms hanging at his sides. After a moment, he took a step closer, took my hand in his and said, 'Will you help me build that wardrobe?'

I nodded, grateful for the distraction.

WHEN I WASN'T WORKING with him on some furniture, or cooking for us, or cleaning up the mess we'd made in the kitchen, I sat in our cherry tree thinking about my old life here, how life had been in Boston, and now was in London. The word *contrast* could not quite describe it. On my last day, my father asked me to kill one of his hens. We were to have

Katherina over for supper and he wanted a feast for his two favourite women. The chicken was in the oven when she stepped through the door. My father's face shone brightly then, and hers lit up too. She approached him and placed her hand on his shoulder. The gentleness, love, and respect between them produced a big lump in my throat, because I knew I would probably never have that.

Katherina came over to me and gave me a hug. 'I'm glad you came. Your father has missed you terribly.'

I could only nod, trying to be very busy peeling potatoes.

THE TRAIN ROLLED into the station to carry me away. My father held me tight, as though this would be our last moment together. But who knew what the future might bring? I soaked up as much of his warmth as I could and tried my best not to weep as I told him that he was the most loving father a child could ever wish for.

The train gave a mighty jerk, belched a blob of steam, and started pulling me north as it hooted Leipzig farewell. I peered out of the window and craned my neck until the small speck that was my father disappeared.

Before I reached Berlin, I knew what I had to do. Tetanus bacteria died on contact with oxygen. I would use sodium sulphite to consume any remaining traces of oxygen in what we had believed to be anoxic culture medium.

Two weeks later, I saw the first colonies appear in my Petri dishes. We used them to infect rabbits and mice. The animals showed muscle spasms a week later. I extended my stay another two weeks to finish my work.

I DISEMBARKED ON JANUARY 16, 1890, glad that the ice hadn't closed off the passage. The additional trunk I carried with me contained a copy of each of the glass cylinders and anaerobic vessels we had developed and used for the cultivation of tetanus germs. I would show them to a glass-blower who would help me supplement my laboratory equipment at Guy's. The trunk also contained my notebooks and the valuable pure cultures, growing inside sealed glass bulbs, carefully wrapped in many layers of cotton and waxed paper.

I had wired Guy's to send someone to safely transport my precious freight from the harbour to the lab. It was late evening when I arrived in London. A hansom cab took me and my companion to the hospital and, after making sure my cultures were safe and undamaged, I went home, happily anticipating my own bed.

Standing at the door to my room, latch key in hand, I hesitated, not knowing what or how many would greet me inside. I shook my head at my own silliness and opened the door.

Twelve heaps were quietly snoring on the floor. The room smelled clean and my bed was untouched. I steered myself there, dropped down, and rolled up like a pickled herring.

12

The following day at noon, I had an appointment with Professor Rowlands — the superintendent of Guy's — and a reporter from *The Times*. I had dreaded this moment of making a show of myself. As I dreaded the upcoming article, which surely would have little to do with what I would say during the predictably interminable interview. Unfortunately, one reporter turned out to be three, a number that grew larger during the course of the day.

It was very late when I finally left the hospital grounds. More than three months of hard work with very little sleep were taking their toll — my head throbbed and I felt sick to the bone. My way home seemed endless, and several times I almost lost my orientation. Eventually, I made it into the small chamber at Bow Street. Lying flat on my stomach, I rested my head on the cold floor and fought the urge to vomit. Once I felt a little better, I rose, replaced my trousers with a dress, and headed home.

It happened as I was walking down Bow Street. A group of young men watched my approach, how I was trying to avoid the mud and puddles of half-melted snow, and failing.

I'd never seen these men before. Not in St Giles or anywhere else. Yet their eyes were glued to me. I looked around, searching for a familiar face, someone who could greet me and prove that I live there, confirm I owned nothing of value except my life.

But there was no one.

All I saw of my neighbours were dark shapes huddled in doorways, drunk from gin or ale, sleeping so soundly that even boxing their shoulders wouldn't have made them stir. Hastily, I crossed the street to increase the distance between the men and me. Six of them. Only one of me. Should they choose to attack, I stood no chance.

The moment they set their legs in motion, my blood began to holler in my ears.

I reached the corner of Endell and Wilson, and began to panic. The streets were empty. The footfalls behind me grew louder. Memories of the rape pushed themselves through my pelvis up into my chest. I almost fainted, which annoyed and shocked me enough to shake off the victim's stupor. I dashed into Broker's Alley and raced as fast as I could, trying to picture a forest around me to make me feel safer or more self-assured. The icy rain needled my face as my feet slammed through ankle-deep puddles.

The clopping of boots on cobblestones quickly approached. Despair cut my breath short. A hand grabbed my coat and yanked. I was thrown onto the street. For a moment, I thought how ironic it would be to drown in a puddle somewhere in London after having crossed the vast Atlantic twice. Almost amused, I realised that they wanted to steal my boots and coat, while ignoring the purse with my money in it.

Then, something hit me on the back of my head. The world began to squeal silently. The boys' shouts were dull throbs and the night turned from a dark grey into screaming red and orange. I could see only flashes of the things happening around me. Someone punched my face and abdomen, but the pain came with delay and felt oddly harmless. The tugging on my clothes and boots didn't matter much to me.

The screeching of a tortured steam engine reached my ears. There was a familiar face — a bear of a man with flaming orange hair was sending boys flying. The street and I were melting into a glutinous and sore mass, as the cold pinched ground and flesh into one. And suddenly I flew.

It took me a while to realise that someone had picked me up and was carrying me away.

I SAW HIS LIPS MOVING, his glistening face. Was there fear in his eyes? My vision was limited and I had the feeling of looking through a narrow tunnel. I meant to speak, but couldn't hear myself make a sound.

Garret had brought me to a place that was unfamiliar to me. He lowered me onto something soft. My ribcage hurt as he did so.

Step by small step, my senses returned. I noticed the cold, wet cloth wiping my face. The back of my head was throbbing so badly, I thought I would be sick. I managed to get my right hand up there and pain shot through my side. I touched the raw mess just above my neck. My fingers pushed and probed, but no bones seemed to shift. Significant fractures of the skull weren't likely. The knowledge relieved me greatly until I noticed that my hand was covered in blood.

'Garret?' I mumbled. 'My head? Look. No touching.'

He turned me gently onto my side. His breathing stuttered. After a long minute, he turned me back again. His face was a mask. 'You need a surgeon.'

'Don't know one.'

'Don' ya act like a maggot, Anna, or I'll eat yer head off!' he barked at me. I flinched and dimly remembered that he always got angry when he felt helpless.

'I'm sorry,' he said softly. 'But you're a nurse, you have colleagues. Someone has to stitch this up.'

I could not think, could not come up with an excuse.

'Will fix it myself. Jus' let me sleep.'

My bones and my head felt so heavy, I started wondering why the bed frame didn't yield. Was there even a bed frame? Garret kept talking to me, but I did not hear much of it. But then an idea crept into my brain. 'Watson. Dr John Watson. Garret, get John Watson.'

'Is he at Guy's?'

'No! No, Baker Street. 221B.'

Garret pressed my hand and disappeared from view.

Sleep carried me away.

~

SOMEONE TOUCHED the raw spot on the back of my head. I woke up to pain that followed suit.

'You have a serious concussion and at least two broken ribs. I'm not sure about further internal damage, but your head wound needs stitches.'

That sounded like Watson. I forced my eyes open, and found three men peering down at me: Garret, Watson, and Holmes.

'Go away,' I mumbled. Exhaustion tugged on my eyelids and all I wanted was peace.

Someone turned me onto my side and began fingering my head. I desperately hoped that Watson knew what he was doing. A hand holding a cup filled with a milky white liquid appeared in front of my face — opium.

'No,' I squeezed out of my dry mouth and pushed the cup away. Only few things could scare me as much as losing control with a chemical substance. I noticed the short, bristly hairs on Watson's hesitating hand, the two cracks at the corners of his thumbnail, a cup that looked familiar. Someone muttered words I didn't understand, then the hand disappeared.

Then came the *snip snip* of scissors as my hair was being cut off around the wound, the clucking noise of liquid pouring out of a small bottle, followed by a sharp, burning pain that told me Watson was disinfecting the back of my head. That was nothing to the pain that followed. It felt as though Watson ripped my scalp off as he joined the torn skin and stitched it together. I bit a hole into my bottom lip, grabbed the hand that was the closest, and squeezed it with as much force as I could muster.

After an endless time of sewing, Watson wrapped my head in bandages. 'Tomorrow morning I'll check the wound and see how you are doing.'

'Hmm...' I answered, noticing a slender hand slipping out of mine.

TWO DAYS LATER, I stood in front of the small glass that hung on the wall of Garret's room. It had taken me hours to realise that I had been here many times before. I was utterly shaken and worried about possible brain injuries and after-effects.

Angling a mirror shard in my hand, examined the back of my head. The bald patch there was as ugly as a scorched forest. The black thread Watson had sewn into my scalp stuck out of the bruised skin. It looked like a barbed wire fence in a battlefield.

I got a pair of scissors and began trimming the dishevelled fringes, but soon noticed that this alone wouldn't do. So I snipped all my black curls off and was left with something that resembled more the haircut of a lice-infested street arab than that of a somewhat orderly adult. Hideous.

Heavy footsteps announced Garret's return just before he knocked on the door.

'For Christ's sake, Garret, will you come in? This is *your* room.'

He rumbled through the door, slammed it shut, and slithered to a halt, his mouth hanging open.

'I know,' I said and turned away, dropping the scissors on a shelf.

He stepped closer and wrapped his big arms around my chest. He whispered my name with an intensity that made my skin go bumpy. I just stood there with my arms hanging limply at my sides, trying to swallow a clump of despair that wouldn't go down.

Garret turned me around and pressed his face into the stubble on my head and told me that I was beautiful. Wrapped up in that bear of a man, who'd always been honest with me, a man I'd never told who I really was, I began hating myself with all my might.

For a long moment, he held me and breathed into my hair. 'You all right?' he asked, and I nodded. He caressed my face with the rough pads of his fingers and fit his mouth on my beaten-up lips. My knees wobbled. He picked me up, carried me to his bed, and laid me down gingerly.

'Do you remember the first night you spent here?' he asked, seating himself on the floor next to me.

I smiled. 'Barely.'

'Ah, well. What about the second night?'

'Was that the night you were convinced I thought of you as Frankenstein's monster?'

'Erm... Yes.'

I sneaked my hand into his, and shut my eyes. 'Now I look like the monster.'

He kissed my fingertips, each and every one of them.

'Garret, I need to tell you something.'

The pressure around my hand increased briefly.

'Come, lay down and warm me a little. I'm freezing cold.' I held up a corner of the blanket, and he moved his large body close to mine. 'Our first night, you asked about the scar, and I didn't want to tell you then. Do you still want to know how I got it?'

'Yes,' he said.

'When I was living in Berlin, and was...' My throat clenched like a fist. But I thought of my father, what he said about loneliness and that he didn't wish that on anyone. I cleared my throat and began anew. 'Three men cornered me in an alley at night. Said I needn't be afraid.'

Garret froze, body and breath.

'They used me. One after the other. But one of them wasn't able to...have an erection. So he used a knife to leave his mark. Not to kill, just to replace one power he did not have with one he had. He wanted to give me a souvenir that would always remind me of him and that night. As if I needed that. As if anyone could forget such a thing.'

He held onto my hand. His fingers were vibrating. 'Is that why you were afraid of me?'

'Yes.'

'That's why you can't bear children? Because he cut you so deep that...' Garret's voice broke.

'No. The wound was too shallow for that. But...I didn't get my monthlies after that. At first I thought...I thought that...'

He kissed a tear off my cheek.

'I was so glad I wasn't pregnant. But I never had my

menstruation after that. Not more than once a year, that is. I don't know why.' I opened my eyes because I needed to look at him. I needed to know if he still saw the same woman in me. The pain and love I found in his face cracked my heart.

'Are they in gaol?' he asked.

'They were never apprehended.' I couldn't tell him that these men and I had studied medicine together, that they had believed I was a man until the night they cornered me to pull a prank and check the size of my prick. And then found there was no prick. I'd never reported them.

Garret propped himself up on his elbow, his mouth a thin slash, the gleam in his eyes brutal. 'I'll kill them. You and I will go to Berlin, and I will kill them.'

Gently, I touched his chest. 'And should I lose you to the gallows? No. Two weeks after the...*incident,* I took my father's shotgun, fit it under my coat, and visited them. I knew where they lived. The one who had used the knife gave me the most trouble. I had to shoot him in his right foot to leave any impression at all. He is still limping. The other two believed me at once when I said I would castrate them if I ever got word they touched a woman without her consent.'

Garret blinked, opened his mouth, and shut it.

'Are you shocked?' I asked quietly.

'Not exactly. I'm... I'm...rather...awed.'

13

I went back home only a few hours later. The moment I closed the door behind me, the realisation hit that I had jeopardised my own future.

For three days I had been sick in bed — Garret's bed, to be precise. Colleagues may have tried to contact me, perhaps to wish me a quick recovery, or to enquire about my return to Guy's. To make matters worse, I was a celebrity now, or close to it. I had made a grave mistake by giving 24 Bow Street as my official address. If anyone had tried to visit, they would have been more than puzzled to find my tiny dressing chamber above a cobbler's.

I lay down on my bed to rest a moment and plan my next steps. I needed a proper haircut. And a new apartment for my life as Dr Anton Kronberg, criminal bacteriologist, might be necessary very soon.

I walked to Bow Street and changed into Anton. A barber wasn't far from there. It felt odd watching him work on my reflection in the glass. With my hair cropped so short, I looked like a man no matter how I dressed. In a way, it was advantageous. Yet it felt like giving up too much of my female identity, and that hurt.

After spending a good part of the day reading advertisements in the newspapers and riding in one cab after another, I finally found a small place in Tottenham Court Road. It was walking distance from my dressing chamber, which would come in useful in case I quickly needed a hiding place.

In the evening, I sent a wire to Guy's, announcing my return to work the following day. It was probably too early, had I asked my head, but it was also rather urgent if I wanted to avoid exposure.

News of a prospective cure for tetanus had spread like fire, thanks to several papers reporting on my work using various mixtures of truth and codswallop. Yet, the news had spread, and I expected a visitor soon — one who wanted me to provide the deadly bacteria for experiments on humans.

ONLY TWO DAYS later that visitor pushed open the doors to my laboratory at Guy's.

'Dr Kronberg?' he said, approaching me with an outstretched hand. Seeing my black eye, he took a step back. 'Why! What *happened* to you?'

'A group of boys mugged me. Not worth mentioning.' I waved his concerns away.

'These thugs are getting bolder every day.' He puffed up his cheeks. His eyes touched on the intricate glassware on my laboratory bench.

'Who are you?'

Taken aback by my lack of courtesy, he blinked. 'My apologies. I didn't introduce myself. I am Dr Gregory Stark, Cambridge Medical School.' He snatched my hand with both of his and shook it heartily. 'We heard about the isolation of tetanus germs, and I wanted to congratulate you personally.'

I nodded my thanks. A strange feeling spread in my stomach — I had heard his name before. Stark was an anatomist, if I remembered correctly. He and I stood almost at eye level. Most men were taller than I, and he had merely an inch advantage. His circumference was roughly three times mine. Despite that, he seemed agile. I guessed him to be around forty-five years of age. His hair had a dark blond or brown colour; it was difficult to define. As was his character. He made an effort to appear kind. But his firm handshake using both his hands somewhat collided with the calculating looks he threw at me and my laboratory. He smiled a lot. It was the grin of an angler fish — always on display, showing a lot of teeth and a bait-like something hanging just in front of the death trap.

'I was in the area,' he continued. 'Visiting an old friend of mine — Professor Rowlands. He told me where to find you. I fancy myself a hobby bacteriologist. You see, the study of anatomy alone does not provide very much excitement or surprises these days.' He chuckled lightly.

Considering Cambridge's history in body trafficking, Dr Stark might just as well have boasted about robbing graves and abducting crawlers. I put a faint smile on my face, one that was supposed to communicate pleasant surprise. And then, my brain produced a nearly audible click.

I flashed him a broad smile of adoration. 'My dear Dr Stark, I know only too well what you mean. I chose my field of research mostly because I believe there are so many discoveries yet to be made in bacteriology.'

He made big watery eyes, and I continued. 'Just think how far bacteriological research advanced with the invention of good light microscopes. It is our tools that limit us today, not our vision. If only we could develop better tests and techniques for studying germs — imagine the greatness we could accomplish!' I poured all my passion for medicine into those words.

Stark caught fire, and he grabbed my shoulder rather too hard. 'Indeed, Dr Kronberg. I feel precisely the same. And yet, so few of us wish to improve our modern methods. So few see our limitations, and the potential for solutions to so many of the problems of mankind, just beyond our arms' reach!' He stretched his free arm as though to snatch at an imaginary something. And he was very happy to have met me.

I beamed, trying to ignore the vice-like grip he had on my shoulder. Did he plan to dislodge the joint?

'I can see we are made of the same material, my friend, if I may call you that?' he said with his warm angler-fish smile.

I forced more enthusiasm into my expression, nodded, and smiled. My shoulder was aching fiercely. The force of his grip made my broken ribs rattle. Or so it felt.

'I hope we can discuss our research and our visions some day?' he asked, and I smiled and nodded some more, now hoping desperately that he would take his paw off me. And he finally did, just before he bade me farewell. He was about to leave my lab when he came to a sudden halt. It seemed a practised move.

He turned and scratched the fur on his chin. 'Dr Kronberg, as I come to think of it now, I can just as well ask you directly. I've been...developing a tetanus vaccine. A very crude one, I must admit. Nonetheless, great efforts have been made, by myself and a handful of brilliant men in Cambridge and London. I was wondering whether...' Here, he looked at me sharply, as though this idea had just hit him. 'I wonder whether you would like to collaborate with us? Your pure cultures could bring swift success to our project, I believe.'

My stomach roiled, I faked surprise. 'I am flattered, Dr Stark. I would certainly be excited to work with an experienced team. But...' I chewed the inside of my cheek, frowned, and let him roast in his own juices for a moment or two.

'Yes?' he said.

'Well, I hope you understand. I've never heard of your project, and I've just been granted research funding to develop my own vaccine. But pray tell, how long have you been working on your vaccine? Perhaps we could...' I shrugged, and let it hang there.

'A few months now. You couldn't have heard about it as we are financing ourselves mostly through private sources. We didn't receive any governmental funding, but you know the problem.'

'Actually, I don't.'

He slipped his hand into his waistcoat pocket and pulled out a watch. 'I must take my leave now. However, let me assure you — the grant you received is a fraction of the funds we have available.' He approached me once more, clapped my sore shoulder, and said. 'Unfortunately, I have other business to attend to now. May I send you an invitation to Cambridge some time soon?'

'I would be delighted.' Sickness spread through my chest. I needed to talk to Holmes today, I thought as I rubbed my shoulder.

TWO HOURS before leaving Guy's, I prepared a wire for Holmes: *Eight o'clock, Wilson & Bow. Got a name for you. Bring your disguise. A.K.'*

Once at home, I quickly ate a sandwich, grabbed the three loaves of bread and two bottles of brandy I had procured for the evening, and went to one of the neighbouring houses. We were to have a party. Although my head didn't feel intact enough for me to dance, I could still enjoy the music and the company for a bit.

A small crowd had already gathered on the ground floor of an abandoned warehouse. The Irish musicians sat on apple crates. I placed the bread and the brandy on a nearby crate, and let the men know that it was payment for their efforts. Grinning, they tipped their hats, and chucked down a helping of their newly won refreshments.

One of them, a smallish fellow with a rake for a haircut, lifted his mug to me and squeaked. 'What butter and whiskey won't cure, is not to be cured at all!'

'I should try that as a new treatment,' I said, eyed the provisions I brought, and added, 'Bloody damn, I forgot the butter.'

Then I remembered that I would not have any patients at all, if I were to work for Stark and his *colleagues*. I would have *test subjects* instead. 'I think I'll be needing a sip of that.'

'Sure,' the oldest of them said, pushing his mug to me. I tipped its contents down my throat, and asked if he had seen Garret.

'The dryshite's over there.' A fiddle bow was poked into the air. Then they began tooting and scratching on their two fiddles, one accordion, and a tin whistle, tuning whatever needed tuning, and arguing about which piece they should play first.

I turned and spotted Garret in a far corner, staring into his ale. The warehouse had filled up. It was still very cold, but the fire in the centre of the large hall, and the dancing, would soon warm up the place. The music started with a blast, and everyone was on their feet, dancing, clapping, laughing, and singing. Surely, standing on an active volcano must feel like this. Despite my sore head and ribcage, and despite Stark's visit and what it would entail, I enjoyed myself.

Garret looked up and his eyes met mine. He seemed to give himself a push before deciding to approach.

'Hello,' was all he said. A frown carved his brow.

'Hello.' I touched his chest and smiled up at him, hoping to brighten his mood.

'What about a dance?'

'I can't.' I rolled my eyes and regretted it instantly when my head started spinning.

He bent over my shoulder and lifted my hat to inspect my wound. 'It's still hurting, isn't it?'

'A little,' I lied.

'You should be in bed.' He tugged a curl behind my ear.

'What makes you so unhappy tonight?' I asked.

He shook his head once.

'Want me to punch someone for you?'

He laughed. 'I just...want to talk to you. And we can dance slow. Outside?'

I nodded, and he took my hand in his and pushed a path through the crowd. Outside on the street, he curled an arm around my waist. I pressed my cheek to his chest, and we danced oddly slow to the fast Irish folk music pulsing through the warehouse walls. When I shivered, he unbuttoned his coat and I snaked my arms inside it.

'So I was thinking that...that...' He halted, and pressed me a little closer, and cleared his thorax. 'We should leave London.'

Stunned, I looked up. 'What?'

'Seeing you like this. Injured. I thought you would...' He pressed his lips into my hair and groaned, 'I can't lose you.'

'I don't want to leave London.'

He huffed. 'I figured.'

A cold wave of resignation was coming off him. It made me sick with worry. 'No arguing today? No asking me why I don't want to leave.?'

He shook his head.

'What is wrong, Garret?' I asked softly.

'You wouldn't tell me anyway. No need asking.'

I was taken aback. 'Only a few days ago I told you a secret I have been dragging around for years.'

'But you're never going to tell me who you are.'

I was about to argue, when he added, 'And you're never going to tell me why you have that thing in your doctor's bag.'

'*Thing?*'

'You have a cock on straps in your bag, Anna. I wonder why you even *have* a doctor's bag. You're a nurse — that's what you tell everyone. What are you doing all day long?' He had disentangled himself from my embrace and taken two steps back. Instantly, the distance between us grew so much, it felt as though we'd never be able to cross it.

'Has it ever occurred to you,' I whispered, 'that I decide whom to trust, and that you can't make that decision for me?'

His jaw dropped. 'You still don't trust me.'

'As you, me.'

He narrowed his eyes. 'What's that cock on straps for?'

'Let us assume I'm a pervert.'

He exhaled a growl, and threw up his hands. He opened his mouth, and shut it, blinked, and said, 'I have work to do.' With that, he turned and left.

I don't know how long I stood there, watching the passing clouds reflected on the puddle before me. Eventually, the cold stung my toes, my head began to spin again, and so I made to leave. After only a few steps, I nearly stumbled over a pile of clothes with a wreck of a beggar inside. 'What are you doing in the middle of the street?' I enquired. He coughed and mumbled something like 'M'lady.'

'Come. Stand up, and I'll help you.' I bent down and offered my hand. The pile started moving reluctantly and a pair of piercing grey eyes gazed up at me.

'For Christ's sake!' I shouted, pulling hard on his tattered coat, almost ripping it in two.

'My apologies,' said Holmes, rising to his feet and looking as though nothing had happened.

'You spied on me!'

'Excuse me, but *you* sent the telegram!' he said, knocking bits of dirt off his clothing.

'I did not invite you to...to... What's the *damn* word again?! ...*eavesdrop!*' I punched his shoulder. 'Damn it, Holmes!' The hard shove hadn't shown much effect.

'I tried to be discreet and give you some privacy. You two almost ran me over. I didn't want to interrupt your conversation, so I quickly took cover and hoped you wouldn't see me. And you would not have, if not for your exorbitant philanthropy!'

'What?'

'Forget what I said. You wanted to give me a name. Whose?'

His swift change of topic didn't go unnoticed and I made a mental note to get the rest out of him later.

'Dr Gregory Stark from Cambridge Medical School is an anatomist who grew...bored. He invited me to take part in a so-called *privately funded vaccine development project.*'

My head was spinning badly now. 'I need to go home,' I muttered and turned to leave. Holmes was at my side instantly, offering me his arm. I took it with reluctance. Oddly enough, he walked me to my apartment without me ever giving him the address. I unlocked the door and he helped me on to my bed.

'Thank you.' I lay down and shut my eyes, hoping I wouldn't vomit on my guest. 'Have you been able to identify the two men?'

'I am very close. I think in two or three days' time I will have found out all there is to know.' After a pause, he added,

'May I ask why you choose to live here? You could easily reside in a better area and still come here every day to treat the poor.'

'Some things are so obvious, and still you can't see them.' I looked up into his face. His eyes darkened. 'Where else could I live with hair as short as mine and not draw attention? Besides, I live here because I *like* it. There is life here. There are real people who speak their minds, quarrel openly and not behind closed doors, who kiss on the streets and not only at home after nightfall. It's dirty, dangerous, and tough to live here, but I prefer this to the controlled boredom of the higher classes.'

I observed his expression but couldn't tell whether he could relate to any of what I'd said.

'A wise decision,' he noted.

'Excuse me?'

'It was wise of you to not reveal yourself to the Irishman, although he was close enough to—'

'Get out!' I hissed. His head jerked back a little as though I had slapped him. Then he rose to his feet, produced a nod, and left with a quiet 'Good night.'

STARK CALLED AGAIN a week after his first visit, and enquired about my bacterial cultures. I told him I would not give out any of them as long as the research paper in *The Lancet* wasn't published. I explained that I was still in the process of characterising several different bacterial strains of the same species, as they seemed to show varying aggressiveness. That was when his eyes lit up.

He wanted to know how the course of the disease differed and was delighted to hear that I had germs that could kill my test rabbits within only three days instead of the expected two weeks. It was a lie, but served its purpose. I also mentioned that additional security measures had been taken to prevent the pure cultures from falling into the wrong hands, which could result in them getting contaminated, or cause harm to the public. But I was keeping all the details secret. Only I knew where and how the cultures were stored and how they were labelled. He tried to hide his disappointment, and renewed his invitation. My hooks were in.

I went home and noticed that my door was unlocked. Slowly, I pushed it open and peeked inside. Holmes sat in my only armchair.

'Do you want me to die prematurely of a heart attack?' I cried.

'I believe you are working on that quite effectively yourself,' he answered calmly.

'Why did you come?'

'I've identified the two victims.'

I shut the door with a bang. 'Pray proceed.'

'The first man was a Scottish farmer, Dougall Jessop, who moved to London roughly four months before his death. His wife died, he lost his farm, and he ended up in the Fulham Road Workhouse. He was on a come-and-go basis, as he had occasional employment outside. In London, he had no friends and no one to miss him. The last they saw of him in Fulham Road was the beginning of summer last year.

'The second man was also a Scotsman, Torrian Noble. He'd lived in London the past five years and spent most of his time in Gray's Inn Road Workhouse, but he too disappeared at the beginning of last summer, and did not return thereafter. Jessop had never set foot into Gray's Inn and Noble was unknown to the Fulham Road Workhouse.'

'So they met in Broadmoor?'

'Likely,' said Holmes.

'How did they get there?'

'I have a theory. Both workhouses belong to Holborn Union, which means they all are being watched by one Board of Guardians, headed by a chairman. I heard from other inmates that a physician had visited to offer treatments, supposedly paid by the Board of Guardians. That was at the beginning of last summer.'

I interrupted him. 'That is most unusual. No such thing as free medical treatment for paupers has ever been provided in any workhouse. At least that I know of.'

'Exactly!' he said. 'My theory is that this physician examines the inmates, interviews them about their family situation, and chooses the ones that have no family, no close friends, and are comparatively healthy. The chairman of the Board of Guardians must be involved. A physician cannot simply walk in and examine paupers at his liking.'

'So both were abducted independently and later managed to escape together. Any idea how Noble got to Guy's?' I asked.

'Unfortunately, I don't. I interviewed a cabbie who drives to Guy's regularly. He said that one day a man approached his hansom who was unable to walk properly and couldn't speak. He grabbed the horse's reins, and sank to the ground. That's what made the horse whinny and rear. The driver believed the man was drunk, cracked his whip, and left in a hurry. He had no idea where the man had come from and he could not remember whether there were any onlookers whatsoever.'

I made tea and sandwiches, and we ate in silence. Then I remembered Stark.

'Stark paid me a second visit today,' I said and Holmes looked up.

'He desperately wants my tetanus cultures. I can expect an invitation to Cambridge any day now.'

'I had hoped that wouldn't be necessary,' he said quietly.

'I'll move into 13 Tottenham Court Road tomorrow and

will give up this place for a while,' I said, waving an arm at my apartment, 'but how will we communicate?'

'You will put a vase or the like into the window of your room whenever you have information that you need to share, or when you are in danger. I will come as soon as possible.'

'When I'm in danger?' I snorted.

'You know what I mean.'

'If you say so. And how will *you* contact me when you need help? By simply walking into my rooms?' I asked, and he nodded.

'And how the deuce will you know when that vase is in the window? Will you be spying on me? Or...are you already?'

He raised an eyebrow.

I groaned. 'So I have a tail now. Splendid. Is that how you knew where I live?'

'No. I asked your Irish friend.'

'Garret would never have told you.'

'He didn't need to tell me anything. After the mugging, I suggested that he fetch clean clothes for you, and he led me to straight to your place without his knowing,' Holmes stated happily.

How very simple. 'And why the bloody hell would you have wanted to know my address?'

'Information of such a nature usually comes in useful at some point or other. As it just has.'

'Next time, just ask,' I murmured.

'You wouldn't have told me.'

'Probably not, no.'

We were quiet for a long moment until Holmes grumbled, 'I don't like it that you throw yourself into the lion's den.'

'I don't like it, either,' I said quietly, trying to hide my fear. It probably didn't work very well. And then it hit me. In the next weeks — months, perhaps — I would put on layers upon layers of disguise. And only one person would know who I was and what I would be doing.

'Holmes?'

'What is it?'

'I know who you are,' I said softly. 'Don't forget who I am.'

He didn't reply, so I turned towards him. He was staring at the ceiling and, at first glance, seemed relaxed. But his face was too still and his hands were rigidly flat on the armrests. Slowly, his face turned towards me, and I explained, 'I will have to shed most of what I am to serve the lie. You may no longer recognise me, but whatever you do see is a part of me.'

14

And since you know you cannot see yourself,
  So well as by reflection, I, your glass,
  Will modestly discover to yourself
  That of yourself which you yet know not of.
W. Shakespeare

March, 1890

The train took me to Cambridge. Or what was left of me. My fears were tucked away safely, as was anything soft that would distract me from my goal. My shirt was starched and crisp, my black coat new from the tailor, and my mind sharp. Wisps of steam flew past the window, occasionally clouding my view of a bleak countryside. The snow had melted two weeks earlier, leaving a muddy black surface behind. No green had dared yet to hatch, and the freezing drizzle poured down from an ever present blanket of grey clouds. One might get the impression the sun would not return this year, but that suited my mood. I pushed that thought aside. Moods were a luxury now that could tip the forced balance of my mind.

The train arrived at Cambridge Railway Station. I walked to an available cab, my heels clicking on the cobblestones, my stick swinging back and forth, my hat pulled low over my face. The cabbie nodded at my order to be driven to Cambridge Medical School. Once inside the carriage, I shut my eyes and exhaled all remnants of tension, imagining a scarlet bull's eye — a goal only I could see and aim at. I wouldn't rest until my bolt had found its centre and blown it apart.

Precisely fourteen minutes later, the cab stopped. I paid the driver without looking at him. Stark was already hurrying across the street, waving one hand in greeting.

He led me into the Great Court of King's College. Its mighty vaulted ceilings with delicate fans of stone criss-crossing like the arteries of a large organism made me think of being swallowed alive. One blink of my eyes and I wiped those surroundings away, focusing instead on the imaginary scarlet spot straight ahead.

Stark opened a door to a small lecture hall. I counted fifteen men wearing stern expressions, aged mostly above fifty, with the older sitting in comfortable armchairs and surrounded by the younger men. Most were smoking and immersed in quiet conversations. Upon our entry, the chatter faded.

My eyes took in the room. It was no ordinary lecture hall. Dark and intricate wood panels decorated the walls. Portraits of more than twenty haughty men, bewigged, robed, and framed in gold, hung all around us.

Stark coughed and every head turned in his direction, all but mine. I kept my gaze canvassing the most distinguished men, trying to identify the leader.

'Gentlemen, it is my pleasure to introduce Dr Anton

Kronberg, England's leading bacteriologist. As you all know, he studied medicine at Leipzig University and took regular internships at Charité in Berlin, where he also defended his thesis. After that, Harvard Medical School awarded him a fellowship.'

A few men nodded approvingly, and Stark continued with a smile. 'Then London had the honour of welcoming him. His work on infectious diseases at Guy's Hospital made him a well-known scientist in all of London's hospitals. But it was his visit to Dr Koch's laboratory in Berlin with his breakthrough in the isolation of tetanus germs that has made him an internationally renowned bacteriologist. His colleagues describe him as driven, hard-working, and highly intelligent.'

Stark turned to face me. 'He has come here today at our invitation, and will give a presentation on his recent work — tetanus, and the isolation and characterisation of the causative agents.'

I inclined my head in acknowledgement and stepped to the podium. I was comfortable giving presentations to much larger audiences and my nervousness usually peaked just before I began to talk, but once standing in front of my exclusively male listeners, I had always felt calm wash over me because I was in disguise. This day, however, I'd felt no nervousness whatsoever. There was nothing but cold drive.

I used a determined and low voice to grab their attention and avoid distracting them with strong variations in pitch or volume. 'My dear colleagues, it is a great honour to speak to you today, here in this lecture hall where the greatest anatomists have spoken before.' I made a sweeping move with my arm, indicating the men in the paintings. 'Yet the topic of my presentation differs very much from those of these men.'

Here I took a few seconds to let the information take effect.

'My field of research — bacteriology — is young, but advancing at unimaginable speed. We bacteriologists deal with the greatest evils for mankind — diseases such as tetanus, cholera, typhoid, anthrax, tuberculosis, and bubonic plague, to name but a few. We study how these diseases spread and how the battle against their causative agents, namely bacteria, can be won. Today, I will focus my talk on tetanus and its recently isolated germs.'

I turned to the blackboard and drew a plot of the numbers of tetanus fatalities in London over the past thirty years. My audience was glued to my lips, as my hand led chalk over slate.

After one hour, my presentation was finished. The men rose to their feet and applauded. Several of the older men approached to shake my hand and congratulate me. Refreshments were offered, and small talk conducted. Then we agreed to meet in a more private setting back in London in three days' time.

I SAT in the tattered armchair of my small, single room apartment in Tottenham Court Road. Leaning far back with my feet on the scarred coffee table, I stared at the ceiling with half-closed eyes. It was the only flat surface in the room that had no wallpaper peeling off. The ceiling was perfectly unremarkable. I hated distraction. Other than that, my emotions were strangers to me. My mind slowly circled around the presentation, the audience, and the visible social bonds and tensions between those men.

STARK CALLED at my apartment three days later, and we took

a private brougham to a destination he wouldn't reveal. I noticed the freshness of the two chestnuts. Their coats were gleaming and dry, and no froth seeped from their mouths.

Thick velveteen curtains remained drawn, but this did not bother me, for I knew London well enough; I walked its streets every day. The journey lasted fifty minutes. Stark chatted, I replied reflexively, following my own thoughts and listening to the noise the wheels made over the ground. At the beginning, it sounded like the broad, flat cobblestones of High Holborn, a large and busy street. The carriage turned right, a smaller street now, followed by the sounds of Blackfriars Bridge and Great Surrey Street. A sharp right turn told me this could only be Waterloo. And, yes, we crossed the river. I used to pass this bridge at least three times every week. I would recognise the rise and fall of it in my sleep. A left turn brought us onto the Strand, with all its bustling and clattering. Then the hooting of a train — we must have reached Charing Cross. Now the brougham turned into Regent Street, Piccadilly, St James, Pall Mall, and then again, and again, going in circles. The pattern changed after a quarter of an hour. At first, I could not sense any familiarity. Maybe I had never been here, or at least not for a long time? But the ducks — the hungry, burred-up, freezing ducks begging for an evening meal from passers-by betrayed the location — we were passing St James's Park on its south side. Then we made a left turn and stopped. This must be somewhere around Kings Road, and south of Palace Gardens.

A large villa revealed itself as our destination. Light poured from its windows onto a brownish lawn. The wind was stiff and old sycamore trees clawed each other with scrawny twigs, their mottled torsos glinting with ice-cold rain. The only green came from artfully trimmed conifers that lined the walkway to the house, and a lichen-covered fountain with water lazily dripping over its rim.

Our heels crunched on the walkway and then we entered the house. Servants took our coats and hats to brush and hang them, while Stark and I made our way across the hall and into a large, panelled smoking room. A fire, crackling merrily, was framed by a mantelpiece of moss-coloured marble. Fifteen men were sitting in burgundy armchairs, smoking, drinking brandy, and taking refreshments from a buffet. No servants were present. This was a meeting in secrecy.

The men received me with handshakes, but not everyone was pleased by my presence. The younger ones shot glances across the room, some insecure, some jealous, some despising. I smiled at them, inclining my head to show a respect I didn't feel. I was completely at ease, for I knew my contribution was essential and they would need my expertise to reach their goals.

A peculiar hierarchy was now apparent. The group revolved around a man with a shock of light grey hair and a bushy moustache of the same colour. I was certain that he was highest in rank. And yet, there seemed to be subgroups that rivalled one another. As the evening grew longer, I came to the conclusion that rank within the smaller groups was based on corruption and intrigue, while the overall leadership was based on power, pressure, and fear. This I could use to my advantage.

The moustachioed man stood. Silence fell.

'Dr Kronberg, you may have heard of me. I am Dr Jarell Bowden.'

I nodded, somewhat surprised that no coldness trickled down my spine.

'I speak for everyone in the room when I say that we are very lucky to have you here.' Men nodded and murmured agreement.

'As Dr Stark has already told you, we were able to obtain

sufficient private funding to conduct research into the development of vaccines.'

Vaccines. Plural. So they must have been experimenting not only with tetanus, but with other diseases, too.

'You correctly stated in your presentation that the successful development of a vaccine greatly depends on the availability of the isolated germs. To be frank, we need your cultures, and we need them soon. And we want you to isolate other germs for us.'

Bowden was used to getting what he wanted, I noticed.

The room fell quiet again and all faces turned to me.

'You honour me, Dr Bowden. But neither will I provide you with deadly bacterial cultures nor agree to isolate more without knowing how they will be used.'

He had not expected such a reply. His shoulders stiffened, his upper lip curled.

I continued. 'You wish to develop vaccines and I have experience in this field. You need my pure cultures, as you've already said. But what then? I don't see anyone in this room able to manipulate them, to grow them, or to produce a vaccine for the necessary test trials on animals and humans. I will only give you the cultures if I have a full and honest understanding of your project, and I am fully included in its work. It will be either that, or nothing.'

I remained standing, my gaze stuck on Bowden's face, and took a sip of brandy. The exquisite taste of smoke and aged oak ran smoothly down my throat.

Bowden sat. All heads turned towards him. Calmly, he gazed at each man in the room. Four men sat stiffly, half turned away from him and me. Then Bowden smiled. It was decided.

~

LATE IN THAT AFTERNOON, I placed a vase in the window of my apartment and boiled water for tea. Half an hour later, a tall man in shabby clothes knocked on my door.

'Come in,' I said before retreating to the far corner of my too small room. 'Sit, please.' I indicated the lonely armchair. A cup of tea on the coffee table was awaiting him. 'I was invited to Cambridge to give a talk on tetanus. A group of sixteen doctors from the Medical Schools of Cambridge and London attended the presentation. Three days later, I met the same group in a villa here in London.'

He took his seat and picked up his cup. I continued. 'Dr Gregory Stark took me there in a private four-wheeler, hoping I wouldn't know where we were going. The curtains were drawn and he involved me in useless small talk. However, I am certain the meeting's location was less than a half mile from Kings Road. I don't know the names of all the men yet, but the leader is a certain Dr Jarell Bowden. I am not sure the house was his.'

He didn't show any sign of recognition upon hearing the name, so I explained, 'Bowden is known for his advancements in sexual surgery on insane women and was suspected of performing cruel and unnecessary experiments on his patients. The charges were soon withdrawn. Bowden had the best lawyer in London. Stark seems to be a senior member, but without much weight. Four of the younger men did not approve of my inclusion in the group. Their names are Hayle Reeks, Ellis Hindle, Davian Kinyon, and Jake Nicolas.'

I pointed to the note lying next to his teacup, with names of six men written on it. 'They all work at London Medical School as anatomists, except for Stark, who is based in Cambridge. It would be good if you could find something that would make it possible to detain the four younger men for a few days, if needed. I might have to get rid of them if they give me any trouble. '

He nodded, and his eyes glazed over as though lost in thought. 'Hum,' he finally said.

'Have you information for me?' I enquired. When no answer came, I walked to the door and opened it in dismissal, staring down at worn floorboards and avoiding his gaze.

He did not move for a long moment. I looked at him then, and saw his eyes darken just before he jumped up and crossed the room in long strides.

He snatched the door handle from my hands and kicked the door shut. 'So you are willing to sacrifice everything for the *greater good?* And simply *get rid* of four men who stand in your way. And then you'll get yourself killed, because that is a neat way to wipe your hands of guilt.' He snapped his fingers and made a noise of disgust in the back of his throat. 'Since when are you so arrogant and simple-minded as to believe martyrdom ever changes anything for the better?'

My breath came out in one long sigh. My balance tipped, slid, and shattered on the floor. My head fell forward as though my neck couldn't support it any longer. The scents of Muscovy and pipe tobacco pull me closer to Holmes.

Shocked, I pushed away from him and walked over to the window, leaning my forehead on the cold glass. The street and the pavement below me were bustling with everyday life. How very far away, I thought. 'If you cannot bear the sight of me, then don't come looking.'

After a long moment of silence, the quiet click of a closing door hauled my self-control back into life. I took the vase, walked down to the street, and gave it to a crawler.

15

The following day, I paid a visit to Superintendent Rowlands to resign my position at Guy's. He'd already heard about the London Medical School's offer to me, and showed no surprise that I'd accepted it. We parted with a firm handshake. Somehow, I had expected more drama.

A few days later, my bacterial pure cultures and I moved into a large and well-equipped laboratory at the Medical School. Two assistants were placed at my disposal to help develop vaccines against the two diseases that were costing London more lives than any other: tetanus and cholera. Compared to these two, the death toll of murderers was negligible.

It took a while to convince my new employers, but at the end of a heated negotiation they agreed that only I — the trained bacteriologist — would handle the hazardous viable bacterial cultures, while my assistants would clean and disinfect laboratory equipment, prepare the culture media, handle heat-killed germs, and record experimental procedures and observations.

For weeks, we tested tetanus bacteria on rabbits and mice

that were kept in the small outdoor area behind my lab. We could reach an immunity of up to fifty per cent — five out of ten animals would not contract tetanus when immunised a week before infection.

Unfortunately, there was a problem with mortality. The heat-killing of the germs was not reliable — one-third of the inoculated animals contracted tetanus and died.

I MISSED Garret so much it hurt. I was sure he hated me now — the short note I had sent him, the gaping hole I had left in his life. Leaving him was the hardest thing I had ever forced myself to do. But I'd seen no other option. If he knew the danger I was in, he would try to save me from it. Not only would that spoil my plans, it could also get him killed. I had nightmares of his corpse floating in the Thames, or finding him shackled on a cot in Broadmoor Lunatic Asylum, or of his severed head presented to me by Stark and Bowden. Waking up from these dreams was not always a relief. I could barely control the urge to run to him.

I sucked in the scent of fresh bread and tried to push Garret from my mind. Standing in my kitchen, I cut two slices off the loaf, spread them with butter and sprinkled a little salt on top, then took the kettle off the flame and poured boiling water onto expensive tea leaves. The hissing gas lamp spread its dim light, sufficient to see what my hands were doing and to let the men down on the street know that I was at home and had not yet retired. This was their sloppy first attempt at spying on me. I had noticed their presence from the moment I left the medical school.

With my sandwich in one hand, I walked towards the small window and cautiously peeked through the tattered curtain. They were arguing in the shadows of a shop window, hands flicking at each other's faces, a fist raised in my direction. That was a good sign. The four who had disapproved of me from day one, also disapproved of one another. I walked down the flight of stairs, opened the door to the street, and called, 'Fancy a cup of tea?'

Their heads snapped in my direction. I stepped aside while holding the door open. They crossed the street, appearing indecisive, almost scared.

'Good evening,' each one of them said, probably not knowing what else would be appropriate. They walked past me and entered the house. I followed and noticed how readily they ascended to the first floor and entered my room. Tonight, I would pull fine silk threads from a handkerchief, and wrap them loosely around the outside door-knob and into the jamb every time I left my room. Anyone trying my door would move the threads from its original position.

I shut the door and blocked it with my body. 'Well?'

The men looked at each other, their faces betraying insecurity. Hindle harrumphed and answered in a defiant tone, 'We don't trust you!'

'Not my problem,' I replied.

'Why do you live in this shabby place?' Reeks asked.

'None of your business. But you are my guests now, and, as your host, I must make an attempt at being polite.' I pulled back my lips and showed my incisors. 'I live humbly because luxury dulls the higher senses. A detail that has certainly slipped your comprehension.'

A fidgeting rolled through them.

'We think you are hiding something from us,' Hindle said, attempting to sound cold and threatening.

I laughed. 'Interesting theory. What information do you have to support it?'

'We talked to your former colleagues at Guy's. Some say

you are soft. You were reportedly treating patients nicer than anyone else.'

I clapped a hand to my mouth in mock terror. 'Horrible! I truly hope you four don't get infected. By the spreading kindness, I mean.' Somewhere in the back of my head I wondered whether I had got suicidal.

Their irritation peaked and the air between us crackled. 'From what we heard, we cannot believe that you would be able to—' Hindle was cut off by Nicolas's elbow making painful contact with his ribcage.

My heart cracked against my ribs. 'Hindle, if you don't trust me, why are you trying to reveal a secret that Nicolas clearly doesn't want me to know?'

Hindle paled. Small beads of sweat appeared on his upper lip despite the chill in my apartment. 'I wasn't... I didn't...'

I interrupted, 'Clearly not, no. Yet, I wonder what Dr Bowden would say?'

Their eyes widened. Good. These men were not Bowden's favourites, and that was precisely the information I needed.

'Gentlemen, I suggest you leave now. Should I ever see you following me again, I will make sure your bloated bodies float in the Thames,' I said softly, opening the door and wishing them a good evening. All four left without protest.

WHEN I ARRIVED at home the following night, I found Holmes sitting in my armchair. Swallowing the shock, I closed the door quietly and pressed my back against it.

His already thin frame had lost considerable weight. He looked haggard and pale, with hollow cheeks and dark shadows under his eyes.

Apparently he noticed my searching look and commented lightly, 'I'm spending most of my time in workhouses. The food there isn't sufficient to sustain even a child, and tastes like paper mill sewage.' He tried a smile. 'But that is of no importance now. Do you know one Mr Samuel Standrincks?'

I shook my head.

'He is the chairman of the Holborn Union Board of Guardians. During the last week, he met with several members of the Club.'

'The *Club?*'

'In lack of a title, I named our group of criminal doctors the Club.' He waved his hand impatiently. 'I overheard a conversation between Standrincks and your dear Dr Stark. A so-called health examination in all of the Holborn Union workhouses will be conducted in one week's time. The Club is about to choose their next test subjects.'

He seemed to be expecting a reply. I did not move a muscle. After a short moment, he said, 'Did you know that Standrincks, as chairman of the Board of Guardians, is paid by the government? The board usually sees very little of the workhouses. It receives reports from committees it appoints. The pay for the committees comes directly from the chairman, who also receives the reports and picks committee members. Every piece of information the board receives is first filtered through Standrincks. And all reports from the board are first passed through Standrincks before they reach the government.'

'Why does one need a board, then?'

'Its sole purpose is to show that the government cares for the poor. Its members receive money and take part in meetings. But as everything passes Standrincks's desk first, their decisions are inconsequential. Needless to say, I will dedicate some time to Mr Standrincks and see whether the government is involved in any way. By the by — how is your research for the Club proceeding?'

Slowly, I shifted my weight from one leg to the other and

answered, 'I am testing the tetanus vaccine on animals. They also want a cholera vaccine, but we lack suitable patients to isolate the germs. I am expecting the Club to deliver one soon, though.'

Holmes's body grew rigid. I guessed it was the coldness in my voice that had thrown him off. I decided to soften it a little. 'We are now reaching the limits of testability. Only after testing our vaccines on human subjects can we say for sure that they are working.'

'You will suggest it?' His voice was flat.

'I may have to. Their actions are still legal.'

'They are tailing you,' he said, cautiously changing the subject. I pulled up one corner of my mouth and answered, 'I know. I'm the newest addition to the Club. They need to make sure they can trust me.' After a short pause, I added, 'It doesn't help that you are here.'

'You underestimate me,' he growled.

'You underestimate me, too.'

'I don't think so. But what you are doing is not healthy.'

I barked a laugh. 'You should see yourself!'

16

When Stark informed me that a suitable cholera specimen had been delivered to my laboratory, I wanted to run the other way. I had known this moment would come, but I wasn't prepared for it. Nauseous, I stared across my room at the small window. The knowledge that ordinary life bustled on behind the dark rectangle gave me only a little strength.

'How was it delivered?' I asked him and *it, it, it* echoed in my brain, bouncing off cold walls like the shrieking of bats.

'Female from Dundee. Transported in a brougham,' answered Stark in telegram style. I made a mental note — Dundee was more than four hundred miles north. How far did the Club's tentacles reach?

'The cabby is a reliable man. We have used him for other such...tasks.' Stark scratched his chin, lost in thought, and I sensed the gaping cleft within the man, one who did not quite trust his young colleague but had been ordered to share sensitive information. 'He was well paid and instructed to disregard any noise she made. We told him she was insane and seriously ill,' he explained. Then he chuckled. 'The man must have whipped his horses like the devil to get here in so short a time!'

Hate boiled up in my chest. I took a measured breath, told my heart to shut up and my fists to uncurl. In my mind, though, I went berserk: I would beat Stark unconscious, and tie his arms and legs with rope. Then I would infect him with cholera and wait a few days. After the disease turned him into an intestine-expelling wreck, I would leave him outside in the cold, lying in his own shit and vomit, without food, water, or even a consoling word for his remaining days. A trial would be the least thing for that monster to worry about.

Fighting for the appropriate amount of curiosity and ease in my voice, I asked, 'Who prepared her for the transfer?'

He stopped short, frowned, but then relaxed. 'A colleague from the Dundee School of Medicine.'

I made another mental note. So the Club had a medical doctor working for them that far away from London. I could only guess how much farther their network reached.

'I dearly hope you took precautions,' I said. 'I shudder to imagine how many have already been involved in this matter — men I probably wouldn't trust to tie their own shoe laces without toppling over.'

A flush of indignation coloured his cheeks. 'Of course, we took precautions! Do you think we are a bunch of imbeciles? The subject has no family. No one will miss her. The driver firmly believes she will receive special treatment at our school.'

His puffed-up chest relaxed. A smile played around the angler fish death trap. 'Do not worry yourself, Dr Kronberg. No one will ever know.' He grabbed my shoulder and squeezed it.

How a man could exude so much hypocrisy and not drop dead of shame was a conundrum to me. 'Did you make sure the disease wasn't transmitted? It's a long way from Dundee.

Chances are, someone made a mistake.' Focusing on avoiding the spreading of cholera and preventing the worst was my dangerously thin connection to sanity. My heart ached like a rotten tooth.

'Really, Dr Kronberg!' Stark shook his head and let go of my shoulder. 'I am beginning to think you trust no one. The interior of the carriage was disinfected by your own assistants. They cleansed themselves thoroughly and were using your new invention — those masks — in addition to wearing aprons and gloves at all times when dealing with the woman.'

I produced an approving nod, and made myself say, 'I will extract the germs before the subject dies.'

We grabbed our coats and took a hansom to the medical school.

As we entered my laboratory, and I spotted a soiled and frail-looking woman lying on the tiled floor — her bony frame half covered by a threadbare blanket, her hands bound behind her back despite her weakness — I felt myself falling apart. I wanted to scream. I wanted to slip a knife between Stark's ribs, and take the woman away from there. My insides roiled as I pulled a mask of calmness over me. I couldn't even count the many layers of pretence anymore. But what did it matter?

Stark and I stepped closer, and that was when I knew she was already dying. Her breathing was so shallow, I barely heard it. Despite the cold, she didn't shiver.

'Leave me alone. You don't want to watch this,' I said.

Stark appeared to have the exact same thought.

WHEN I UNTIED HER HANDS, her ribcage began to heave. Convulsions shook her. Her unsteady gaze found me kneeling next to her. Her eyes drifted in and out of focus. She opened her mouth, but was unable to speak. I took her cold and shrivelled hands into mine, as though I could give her enough of my warmth to help her back to life.

'I am so sorry,' I choked.

Her legs began to twitch. The loss of fluids and minerals was causing her muscles to contract uncontrollably and painfully. Her eyes watered. And I sensed it then, the end. And wished I could be the one taken away. How stupid of me to think I could haggle with Death.

I held both her hands in one of mine, and stretched up to take a bottle of ether from the shelf above me. I poured a large amount onto a handkerchief. I wished I could ask for her permission, but it seemed as though she couldn't even perceive her surroundings. I hated what must come next, hated it so fiercely that my body shook. I felt removed from myself, from reality, and from all that once had mattered to me. Panting, I pressed the stinking cloth against her mouth and caressed her soiled hair until long after her heart had given up fluttering.

I DISINFECTED MY HANDS, arms and face, put on my gloves, my mask, and apron. Then I inserted a narrow tube into the woman's rectum, connected the other end to a large syringe, and extracted about a quarter ounce of dirty greenish fluid.

Carefully, I spread drops of it onto dishes of fresh culture medium my assistants had prepared. Half of the Petri dishes were kept under the exclusion of oxygen, the other half with air contact — I wasn't certain whether cholera germs grew under oxic or anoxic conditions.

I poured the remaining fluid into a beaker and heated it to eighty degrees Celsius for twenty minutes. After it had cooled down, I fed it to half the mice and rabbits, and marked them by shaving a bit of fur off their bellies. No one would notice, I hoped. With extraordinary luck, I might be able to obtain a cholera vaccine without the Club's knowledge. Perhaps it could help save lives. Perhaps it could pay for what I'd done.

After I washed and disinfected my hands, I prepared a letter — a small piece of parchment in a cheap envelope — that would be mailed the next morning to Mr Sherlock Holmes, 221B Baker Street:

Guilty of abduction, torture, and neglect of an unidentified female cholera victim, deceased today at London Medical School: Dr Gregory Stark, Dr Jarell Bowden, Assistant Mr Daniel Strowbridge, Assistant Mr Edison Bonsell, and an unknown medical doctor from the Dundee School of Medicine. Guilty of murder of the same woman: Dr Anton Kronberg.

17

When Dr Jarell Bowden called at my quarters the next evening, I was sure I would die. I threw a glimpse over his shoulder, expecting a man to jump from the shadows any moment, to put an end to me with a neat little knife, or a pair of calloused hands around my throat.

Bowden noticed my hesitation and cleared his throat. Hastily, I gifted him a hint of a bow, trying to convey how very honoured I felt by his presence, beckoned him in and offered him my only armchair. Bowden took the tattered seat with reluctance. It had once been a burgundy red, but time had turned it dull pink, except for the patches, which were almost white now.

I couldn't fathom why he was here. Had someone watched me the previous night? I had shown emotions, yes, but I doubted anyone could have done what I'd done without breaking down. Trembling, I poured tea and moved a chair to the other side of the coffee table. Bowden's expression was controlled, but his eyes darted here and there, taking in the shabby furniture, peeling wallpaper, and limited space. He couldn't hide a sneer.

'How may I help you, Dr Bowden?' I sat down, my heart kicking my ribs so hard I worried he might hear it.

'I understand you threatened four of my men,' he said. Only then did he take his eyes off the room, and narrowed them at me. 'Is that true?'

I wanted to weep with relief. As long as Bowden openly confronted me, I was safe.

'Absolutely,' I answered.

Bowden's body gave the slightest jerk backward, his eyelids flickered once. 'You do not even defend yourself?'

'I feel no need to do so. They followed me to my home. Apparently without your orders, because when I told them I would inform you about this, they seemed scared. They informed me that they don't trust me. Hardly surprising. I couldn't care less about their tiddly feelings, and I believe that had you wished to spy on me, you wouldn't have assigned those four bumblers.'

Bowden showed no reaction to my disparaging statements, so I continued. 'One of them was about to reveal a secret that was not for me to know.'

He raised his eyebrows, but managed to pull them down soon enough. Was he aware of my scrutinising gaze?

'They behaved like dumb school children. Their actions were not thought through, their planning nonexistent.' I placed my cup on the saucer. The soft *clink* was followed by Bowden clearing his throat. Before he could speak, I said, 'They put feeling above knowing, and followed a hunch. This is not only disgusting, but presents a serious threat to our endeavour. So I told them that I would shove them into the Thames if anything like that were to ever happen again.'

'They told me a different story,' he responded lightly.

'It falls to you to decide whom to believe.' I twitched a shoulder and forced my mind to think only of the scarlet bull's eye. I did not move, nor did I take my eyes off my guest.

After a long moment of consideration, he said, 'You strike me as rather odd. Any other man would have tried to convince me of his innocence and would have fought to gain my trust. Why don't you?'

Goosebumps crawled over my skin. 'It is because I do not put words above actions. If I were in your position, I would not trust that new man, either. And you don't, which makes you a safe leader. I would put a tail on the man. I would ask his former colleagues what kind of person he is. You took these precautions and I respect you for that. At some point, though, I would have to make a decision. Either I can or cannot trust him. At some point, I would have to take a risk. It's either in or out. As the leader, you have to make that decision. Only you can know whether those four men have always been trustworthy to the highest degree, have never lied to you, have never done anything that could have jeopardised your goals. I am in no position to recommend which action is the one you should take, Dr Bowden.'

Silently we gazed into each other's eyes. After a long moment, Bowden pouted his lips and produced a scant nod. 'I have never met anyone who speaks so openly. I must warn you. You are very close to being subordinate and disrespectful. However, I will think about our problem and will, as you have correctly surmised, keep you under surveillance for the time being.'

With that, he took his leave. After the door closed, I pressed my aching head into my palms and sat on the chair for a very long time, all the while thinking of my dead body floating face down the Thames.

ANNELIE WENDEBERG

THE WOMAN from Dundee walked into my room. Without emotion, she gazed at me. I lay in my bed, unable to move. She lifted my blanket and crawled in next to me. 'Sleep, Anna,' she said softly, as she placed her skeletal hand, which was neither warm nor cold, onto my chest. She smiled then. Her hand was heavy, a rock crushing my lungs. I couldn't move. She was smiling still, and I was dying.

Greedily I sucked in the cold air, hurled myself out of bed, and vomited into the chamberpot.

~

SHAKING WITH WEAKNESS, I went to the door to call to Mrs Wimbush, my landlady. I didn't wait for her reply, but made my long way back to bed and wrapped my freezing body in blankets. Sleep came fast, and relieved me of stomach ache and nausea.

Someone harrumphed. I opened my eyes and saw Mrs Wimbush standing next to the bed.

She appeared slightly annoyed. 'What's wrong? You're poorly?'

'I believe I've contracted cholera. Please don't touch anything, but if you have, wash your hands with a lot of soap.'

Her eyes widened, and she moved back a few inches.

'Mrs Wimbush, I would be ever so grateful if you could fetch clean water, lots of it. And a large chamberpot, please...' I saw Mrs Wimbush wrinkle her nose. 'And would you please prepare a mix of freshly chopped onions with black pepper? A pound would suffice, I think. Grind it together to a paste. Fresh lime would be very helpful, too, so I can mix it into my tea. I will also need potassium permanganate from the apothecary to disinfect the diarrhoea before either you or the maid touch the chamberpot.'

'I.. I shall...' she whispered, rather pale now, '...call for a doctor.'

'No! Thank you, Mrs Wimbush, I am a medical doctor and can take care of myself. But I would be very grateful for a good fire.'

The last thing I needed was some quack who examine me and find the odd details of my anatomy.

Mrs Wimbush squinted, scratched the sparse hair on her chin, and then left the room. Soon she returned with the requested chamberpot, and coal for a respectable fire.

AROUND NOON, my landlady brought most of the things I'd asked for. During her absence, I meandered between bed and chamberpot, alternating between vomiting, half-consciousness, and explosive diarrhoea.

Inside, I felt ice cold, while my skin burned with a high fever. I was sweating profusely. It felt as though my body wanted to get rid of all the liquids it had stored. I imagined myself shrivelling up like a stranded jellyfish in the sun.

My wrapped-up breasts were beginning to ache. But I could do nothing about it, as Mrs Wimbush was walking in and out of my room, exchanging chamberpots and soiled sheets every so often. Two small bulges beneath my sweaty shirt would have been more than obvious, so they had to stay in confinement.

Once she offered to send the maid to help me wash. I refused, hoping that she would take my protest seriously, and not write it off as the ramblings of someone too sick to think.

It took two days of drifting in and out of consciousness, expelling bodily fluids, and wishing to die rather sooner than later, before my strength finally returned.

When I found the energy to wash, I bolted my door, shed my nightshirt, and undid the bindings around my chest. It left me out of breath.

Warm water was waiting in the ewer next to the wash-bowl, and I scrubbed my reeking body. It took two changes of fresh water to finally feel clean again. Panting and naked, I sat down in my armchair and let the blazing fire toast my front.

BY MORNING of the third day, I felt my appetite return. The bits of dry bread I'd had for breakfast had not come back up my throat, and so I knew that cholera lay behind me.

Just as I undressed and started to wash the night sweat off, I heard a knock on my door.

'Who is it?'

'Mrs Wimbush, havin' a telegram for you,' she shouted a little too loud through the closed door.

'Thank you, Mrs Wimbush. Could you please leave it at the top of the stairs? I am not fully dressed at the moment.'

She harrumphed — I assumed in the affirmative — and stomped down the stairs.

I waited until I heard her door slam shut, then opened mine a small crack and snatched the wire. Its content made my neck tingle.

WILL CALL TONIGHT AT SEVEN. J. Bowden.

I STARED down at the piece of paper, hoping the letters would disappear. Unfortunately, they did not.

I wasn't ready for Bowden. My mind felt as thick as honey. The only person I could think of now, the only one who might know what to do, was Holmes. So I put my teapot in the window as a sign for him to come. I had barely washed and dressed when a rap on the door announced his arrival.

I opened and Holmes entered, in pauper attire and work-house stench.

'Good Lord! What happened to you?' he said as I shut the door.

'Cholera,' I said, retreated to my armchair, and placed my cold feet close to the fire. I had seen myself in the glass earlier — my already gaunt complexion had transformed to a rather famished look with dark shadows under my eyes, scaring even me.

He exhaled a loud huff. 'Why the deuce did you not call me earlier?'

'Because I know how to treat cholera, and you don't,' I offered as an explanation.

He mumbled something like 'pigheadedness,' then said, 'I must have a word with my street arabs. They should have notified me earlier.'

'Notified you earlier of what?'

'How many days have you been sick?'

'A few,' I answered.

'And not left this house,' he said, walking to my window and peeking through a gap in the curtain. 'The boys are lazily sitting on their bums, observe you neither coming nor going, and think nothing of it!'

Abruptly, he turned. 'And how can I be of service today?' Sarcasm cut through his voice.

I frowned and was about to give him the wire, when I noticed the state of his hands.

'How long have you been picking oakum?' I asked. He didn't answer.

I fetched a pair of forceps from my doctor's bag.

'Sit.' I motioned to the armchair and sat next to him on the armrest. Awkwardly, I took his hands and started extracting oakum shrapnel from his skin.

'How odd,' I said softly. 'No one notices that your hands

are not used to hard work, that workhouse stench doesn't cover the smell of Muscovy soap and tobacco, that you have a decent haircut, that your ears are clean, that you have shaved with a sharp blade, that...'

'It never fails to surprise,' said he while I pulled a particularly thick splinter from beneath his thumbnail. He didn't even flinch.

'It never surprises me that people can't see *me*,' I answered, and saw his expression flicker from quizzical to nonplussed, before he put his mask back on.

I was done with the splinter extraction, and let go of his hand. 'Bowden sent me a telegram. He will call tonight. I don't know what he wants, but it can't be anything good.'

I stood and rummaged in a drawer until I found a small jar with a thick yellow paste in it. Silently, I worked it into Holmes's hands until he smelled like a flock of sheep.

'Lanolin helps the skin heal quickly, and it has mild antibacterial qualities.' I released him then and looked into his face. 'I'm not ready for Bowden. I can barely think, and I certainly won't be able to act my part.'

I didn't mention that I was about to panic, but I guessed it hadn't escaped his notice.

'Bowden knows you've been ill?'

'He does. I asked the housekeeper to send a wire to the medical school three days ago.'

'And you really can't think of anything he might want other than to have you back in your laboratory?'

I shook my head.

Holmes rose and waved his arm for me to sit. 'If Bowden knows you've been seriously ill, he will not be surprised to see that you are not yourself. You can pretend to feel weaker than you really are. Stay in bed when he calls, shut your eyes often, breathe heavily, etcetera. You are an excellent actress, you are intelligent, observant, and you can adapt to any situation. You need to put more trust in your own skills.'

'Holmes,' I said, and my voice was about to break. I cleared my throat and pulled myself together. 'I am asking you for help. When have I ever done that? I do not have the nerve to face Bowden today. I will jeopardise our investigation.' *And probably get myself killed*, I added silently.

'Hmm...' he grumbled. 'A grave situation.'

A moment later, he clapped his hands together, eyes shining, and told me not to worry myself, to go to bed and find some rest.

'What's the plan?' I asked his back, which was almost out the door.

He turned and stuck his face through the open crack, produced a boyish smile, and answered, 'A hold-up is the plan. Bowden will find it impossible to pay you a visit tonight.'

The door snapped shut. Groaning, I leant back in my armchair and closed my eyes. 'It's probably asking too much for a non-cryptic explanation.'

18

I stood in front of the glass, facing myself. To truly face ourselves, to behold the real person, is the hardest thing in the world. I dared face myself that day for one heartbeat only. Then, I turned away to enter the world of Dr Anton Kronberg.

IT TOOK me a considerable time to get dressed, walk down into the street, and find a cab to the medical school. My forehead itched with cold perspiration. I took my seat in the carriage, wrapped a blanket around my legs, and condemned my weakness. The timing was more than inconvenient.

My two assistants were busy preparing a fresh batch of media when I entered the laboratory. Everyone adhered to etiquette — I bade them a good morning and they politely enquired about my health.

However, the surveillance had fortified — the two men were keeping within three yards of me. I struck a match on the table and lit the Bunsen burner, and wondered how much time I had left.

Using a magnifying glass, I inspected the colonies growing on the solid media. The Petri dishes clinked quietly as I pushed them about, opening and closing their lids, checking their contents. My two assistants were quietly observing my doings, their stares boring into my neck and making my skin tingle.

I found bacterial colonies in a vast diversity of shapes and colours under both oxic and anoxic conditions. We would need a lot of mice to test them on. 'Mr Strowbridge,' I said without turning. 'We will need at least one hundred mice to test the new cultures. I want you to procure them immediately. And supplement the cages and the fodder, please.' I kept my voice feeble to reflect my supposed weakened state. It wasn't much of an act.

Strowbridge nodded and left. Bonsell stayed behind, and moved a bit closer to compensate for his lack of a colleague. Several minutes after Strowbridge had gone, faint footfalls sounded in the hallway. I hoped it would be Bowden. Meanwhile, Bonsell had squeezed himself a little too close.

'Mr Bonsell, you seem to believe you are resistant to cholera.' I held a slender iron lance into the Bunsen burner's flame, just above the hottest blue. 'I know you are supposed to keep an eye on me,' I said softly, pushing the glowing lance into the solid media. The hiss made him jump. 'But you are overdoing it. I might stumble over you and accidentally poke this lance in your neck.'

'You are mad.' He took a step back.

I placed the lance on the bench and turned. 'No, *you* are. The way you handled that woman was more than unprofessional. You've trailed her highly contagious faeces across my laboratory, risking not only the contamination of my valuable pure cultures, but the spreading of a dangerous disease. I contained it at a high cost to myself. I will no longer accept your foolishness.' I rose to my feet, and put my face close to Bonsell's. 'The sooner I am rid of you, the better.'

'Well, well, Dr Kronberg,' interrupted Bowden as he entered the room.

I dropped my gaze, knowing he had overheard us. The charade had been played solely for him.

'Mr Bonsell will give us a moment of privacy,' said Bowden, without looking at the man. He positioned himself to my right, arms crossed over his chest, eyes black like the fetid mud of a Thames's bank. I sat back down and let him tower over me.

'How far did you advance with the pure cultures?' he asked.

'I have obtained a number of isolates that need to be characterised and identified. Strowbridge is procuring mice this very moment. I'll use them to test the cultures, and in no more than five days, we should be able to tell which ones are the cholera germs. After that, I will grow the amount you require.'

Bowden merely inclined his head. He took a step closer, and I forced myself to meet his gaze. It took some effort. His eyes made me feel like I was drowning in tar.

'How is it that you contracted cholera? Shouldn't you, of all people, know how to avoid that?'

'One would expect so, yes. However, it was inevitable.'

'I don't understand,' responded Bowden to my cryptic statement.

'My two assistants brought in a dying woman and smeared a trail of her contagious faeces from the entrance all through my laboratory. That left me with two options — fume the room with concentrated acid and sacrifice not only the usability of the subject, but also my tetanus cultures. Or scour the floor. Naturally, I chose the latter.'

'You could have told them,' he jerked his head towards the door, 'to do it for you.'

'Excuse me, but have they not proved themselves unreliable?'

Bowden's eyes narrowed and he contemplated for a moment. Then he leaned forward and rasped, 'What, in your opinion, should we be doing with the isolated cholera germs?'

I stared into the flame. In contrast to all other fires, a Bunsen burner's flame is perfectly steady. My answer would most likely decide whether I would survive the day.

I swallowed the possibility of a very short life span and answered calmly, 'I can only guess, Dr Bowden. But the fact that you abducted a cholera victim must raise the impression that you are a man without scruples.'

The blood vessels in his throat hectically tapped beneath the skin, blood rose to his cheeks, and his mouth compressed to a slash.

I smiled. 'I admire that.'

Slowly, the colour drained from his face and I added, 'You are well aware that *my* neck is already in *your* noose. I euthanised the woman. That might be interpreted as manslaughter, but more likely as murder. How often do I have to prove my trustworthiness, Dr Bowden?' I tried to keep most of the rage out of my voice. Just a little remained audible, to let him taste my impatience.

'I repeat my question: What should we be doing with your pure cultures?'

I saw the door of opportunity open wide. 'Test both germs and vaccines on human subjects,' I replied.

Bowden's expression relaxed, but there was still a trace of doubt in his eyes. I took a deep plunge into the black and let my imagination go rampant. 'Considering that the Kaiser may be planning a war, I would try to develop highly aggressive strains of pathogenic bacteria to use in systematic germ warfare.'

It was an insane idea, a wild guess, something to press the point that I had absolutely no scruples.

And it had the desired effect. Bowden was thunderstruck.

19

On a rainy Wednesday morning, Stark and I met with Mr Standrincks, chairman of the Holborn Union Board of Guardians. Standrincks was to distribute contracts in all of Holborn's workhouses — harmless-looking sheets of paper that allowed the testing of novel vaccines on inmates — to be signed by men, women, and children willing to take part in our trials. Most of these people couldn't read at all, or well enough to understand the small clause at the very bottom of the contract that permitted the Club to inject a mixture of active bacteria of their choosing to test the efficacy of immunisation.

None of the paupers knew they were about to sign their own lives away for the pitiful price of two sovereigns. As it was the poorest of London who were to receive money in exchange for a small prick in their biceps or for swallowing a spoonful of liquid, we could expect a large number of volunteers to choose from.

After our meeting in Standrincks's office, we took a four-wheeler to inspect Fulham Road's workhouse. The selection process was to begin the next day.

THE VASE WAS SITTING on my coffee table when I returned home late that evening. It was like a slap in the face. I stood frozen in the doorway and only reluctantly moved forward, gazing into every corner. But the room was empty.

I stared at the vase, not daring to touch it, let alone toss it out of the window. I knew too well what it meant.

Two sharp raps and Holmes entered without waiting for my invitation.

He shut the door, leant against it, and said casually, 'I saw you today. Needless to say, I want you to select me for the trial.'

My guard fell. 'No,' I breathed, and turned away from him to look out the window. My eyes burned.

Soft footfalls on the floorboards, a creak, then another — this time, closer. 'I was under the impression that we have the same goal. How else can I appear in court to testify?'

'The tests are legal. We will give out contracts for signed consent.' My voice reflected back into the room. The glass I had spoken to clouded. I turned to face him. My hands grabbed the windowsill for support.

He was quiet for a moment, rubbing his forehead.

'I am sorry. I wish...' I dropped my gaze to his threadbare shoes. Coarse wool stockings peeked through various holes. 'I wish I could end this now.' I waved my own remark away, impatiently and almost ashamed of its uselessness.

'Does Bowden trust you now?'

'Not entirely. But I do hope he believes I'm worse than anyone in the Club.' I avoided looking into Holmes's eyes.

'What did you do?'

'It's a long story. I'll tell you when this is over.'

'You must choose me for the trial.'

I snorted. 'Make me.'

'And you'll have to find a way to avoid killing dozens of people,' he spat across the room.

'What do you think I'm doing, Holmes? Do I look like I'm enjoying myself?'

'Hmm... perhaps you are.' He took three strides forward to pluck at my newly tailored waistcoat. 'Well made, finest materials. Expensive, I dare say.'

Furious, I slapped his hand away. 'You need to come up with something better to make me hate enough to send you off to get injected with tetanus or fed cholera!'

Calm grey eyes met mine when he said softly, 'I'd very much prefer if you'd not have romantic feelings for me.'

'What?'

He huffed. 'What else would it be? You get soft around me.'

'It's called *empathy*, not flirting. For Christ's sake Holmes!'

He still stood close to me, closer than I found comfortable.

'I believe I am correct.'

'This discussion is pointless.'

'I do hope so. Have a good night.' With that, he left.

Damn me to hell and back if he hadn't touched upon the truth.

STARK and I stood in the large dining hall of Fulham Road's workhouse. The vaulted ceilings were reminiscent of a church, but the odour wasn't. A stink of stale porridge and sweat, bleach, mould and dust was carried along by cold air creeping along stone walls.

The inmates were dressed in their best attire for the occasion. The women wore clean dresses, white aprons, and neat caps; men were clad in greater variety, suited for their work:

Those from the shoe shop wore leather aprons, heavy trousers and boots. Those from the farm had on equally sturdy outdoor wear. All of them were exceptionally clean. They wanted to look appealing. It weighed my heart down to watch them as they lined up, eager to sign the consent.

Fifty subjects had been selected from a much larger number of volunteers. These should suffice for the first tests. The day before, I had convinced Bowden that I would have the final word in the selection process. Strong and healthy adults were what we wanted; no children, no old or undernourished people, no pregnant or nursing women. The mortality rate might be higher in those groups and dead paupers would raise suspicion, I had argued. Bowden had agreed.

With each pauper I examined, Holmes moved closer and closer in line. For more than half an hour I had avoided his gaze until finally he stood before me, holding the signed contract in his outstretched hand.

My fingers ran over his biceps and ribs, I pulled the lower lids down to check the colour of his eyeballs, and said dismissively, 'Not this one,' to Stark without ever addressing the man in front of me.

'Why? He looks comparatively healthy,' was Stark's surprised answer.

'Too old and undernourished. I will not use him.' I pushed Holmes aside. The ordeal had aged him.

'Next one!' I called out, knowing I could expect a visitor that night.

20

Holmes never appeared. Perhaps he had found another solution, so that his taking part in the test trial was no longer necessary. And after all, who was he to order me around?

But he was not to be found at Fulham's, nor in two other workhouses we inspected the following day. After yet another night, I got so worried about his well-being that I placed the vase in the window.

But no one came.

THE CHANGE of climate in my laboratory was palpable. My two assistants were more cooperative than ever. Although the surveillance was still in effect, my room to manoeuvre had widened considerably.

'Strowbridge, I need to talk to Dr Bowden. Send him a wire, if you please,' I said the moment I entered the laboratory early the next morning.

Strowbridge nodded and left at once. Now, it was only Bonsell in the room, and he was the less observant of my two assistants.

I picked up two beakers that contained liquid pure cultures of cholera germs, and carried them over to my workbench. We would need both active and heat-inactivated bacteria for the tests on human subjects. My assistants had cleaned and sterilised four flasks for this purpose, and I would fill and seal the vessels now for use the next day.

'Mr Bonsell, would you give me a hand?'

He approached and eyed the liquid cultures standing next to a lit Bunsen burner.

'Careful, they are active,' I warned. A sideways glance at Bonsell's hands told me that my words were having the desired effect. He was stiff as a board.

'Use these empty Petri dishes to cover the beakers, then place the cultures into the water bath. Keep them there for two hours at exactly eighty degrees Celsius. In the meantime, I will prepare the active germs.'

Bonsell nodded. He did not know that our process for producing vaccines called for just twenty minutes of heat inactivation, to kill germs but leave some of their cell characteristics intact. This was too risky an undertaking. Any surviving germ could cause an infection, and ultimately, death. I didn't mind dead mice, but I wouldn't risk killing people with my concoctions.

So I made sure that the cultures would be boiled to death and no lives would be endangered.

Bonsell picked up the beakers. The liquid inside quivered in unison with his hands.

'Pull yourself together, man! The germs are in a bottle. They won't *jump* at you.'

His eyes shot to me and back to the flasks before he took

the Petri dishes and placed them carefully on the beakers' mouths. The liquid shook and the glass made little clonking noises as he carried them over to the water bath. As soon as he had turned his back to me, I started to count down from twenty.

Quickly and carefully, as I had already done with the tetanus bacilli, I plugged the bottles containing the active cholera cultures with a rubber stopper and made sure the seal was very tight — *sixteen.* I opened my bag — *eleven* — removed two identical bottles — *eight* — and placed them on the lab bench — *five.* Then I slipped the bottles filled with active cholera germs into two separate leather bags inside my doctor's bag — *two.* At home, I would add a large amount of creosote to render them harmless, and then pour them into the Thames.

A heartbeat later, I was back under Bonsell's surveillance. Strowbridge returned not ten minutes later, Bowden's answer in his hand:

Will call tonight, six o'clock, your quarters, J.B.

I POURED BOILING water onto tea leaves and placed two cups and the teapot on the coffee table. The armchair was for Bowden, my one kitchen chair was for me. The bell announced his arrival. I opened and beckoned him in.

'Thank you for coming, Dr Bowden. Please take a seat. May I offer you a drop of tea?'

He nodded and inspected the cup before taking a cautious sip. The *click* of the cup set back onto its saucer coincided with his expectant gaze catching mine. It felt like a knife to my throat.

'The cholera cultures are ready,' I began. 'I prepared

enough liquid of both active and heat-killed bacteria to test tomorrow, if you so choose. However, I must caution that we must use them within two days. If kept in this state for too long, they will be rendered ineffective.'

Bowden lowered his head in acknowledgement. He hadn't spoken a word yet. Slowly, I let myself relax against the back of my chair. The backrest produced a squeal. 'Do you wish me to tell you what we should be doing next?'

Bowden's mouth twitched at the corners, his pupils widening to their usual threatening black.

'Dr Bowden, I know you trust me about this far.' I held up my right hand, thumb and index finger almost touching. 'But remember, I can be convicted for what I have done for you. I am honest with you. So honest, in fact, that it shocks you. Still, you cannot come to a decision, whether to trust me or not. Why is that?'

'You are German.'

I couldn't help but bark a laugh. 'Well, that is neither my fault nor should it be a problem. England is my home. I have very few fond memories of my life back in Germany.'

Bowden did not move. He only smiled.

'Again, a decision I cannot make for you. I'm growing tired, Dr Bowden. I have come to the conclusion that you chose subjects for the cholera trial without my knowing it. And you did so several days ago.'

He lost his smirk.

'I am not stupid. That is, after all, why you chose me in the first place. I noticed that a few paupers had disappeared from the workhouses. It seemed to me that those who vanished were those that I'd found lacking, yet Stark believed to be of sufficient strength. Twenty subjects, if I've counted correctly. Ten men and ten women. You had them moved to a secret location because you want to infect them with cholera and you can't do so under all the eyes of London.'

My gaze was stuck to Bowden's face. Gradually, he released all air his lungs contained. His body moulded itself comfortably into the gentle curves of my armchair.

'It is time I introduce you to Broadmoor.' He sounded relieved as he said it.

'Hum. I know Broadmoor and Nicholson. He is a driven man and seems a good choice. He has no scruples, nor any other moral baggage,' I replied, trying to calm my frantic heart.

After the second cup of tea and the exchange of pleasantries, we agreed to take Bowden's brougham to Broadmoor early the next morning.

Bowden led the way as we crossed Broadmoor's courtyard and aimed for the high security blocks. 'We chose a set of twenty subjects,' he said, 'as you correctly observed.'

I remembered the place, the fear, and the night spent under a tree. With haste, I flicked the memory away.

We walked through a large hall, its cold stone walls echoing our footsteps. We passed twenty small cots, each equipped with four fetters. Interwoven with the sharp *clack clack* of our heels was a quiet murmur; it seeped from the back of the hall and announced the dawn of horror.

I made for the noise, Bowden in my wake. We passed through an arched doorway and a narrow corridor that forked like a snake's tongue. At the tip of each fork was an iron door with a peephole.

I aimed towards the left and stood on tiptoe to look through the opening. Ten women, aged approximately between fifteen and forty, were squeezed together in a small cell. A bucket that served as a privy was full to the brim. I could taste the stink of fear at the back of my throat.

With foreboding so heavy I could barely walk, I made for the door to the right. That room harboured ten men. My heartbeat was a thunderstorm, but I didn't hear it. I didn't see the door, or the cell, or the other inmates. All I could see was this one man. And I felt my armour peeling off, like a skin too small and too brittle to be worn any longer.

Somewhere in Berkshire, an oriole male cried his melodic call, and the raspy answer of the female followed soon after.

21

Clarity of mind means clarity of passion, too; this is why a great and clear mind loves ardently and sees distinctly what love is.

    B. Pascal

It was only a short glance that he cast at the iron door, at my eye in the peephole. Then he retreated into a corner, sat, and picked at his socks. The thought of the dying rabbits and mice behind my lab at the London Medical School sneaked into my brain, threatening to blow it apart. Our time had run out.

Someone behind me spoke; it was Bowden. My throat was clenched like a fist, my mouth was a desert. He tapped my shoulder and slowly, I turned around, trying to conceal my rage. My brain sent an urgent command to my lungs to resume breathing. Not so much for oxygen, but to avoid discovery.

I coughed and looked at Bowden. 'They look too sick already!' I barked at him.

His expression hardened. 'These are the only ones available! Use them.'

'When do we start?' I strained to put only curiosity in my voice, and not the stampede of angst and hate.

'Tomorrow.'

∿

THE FOLLOWING DAY, a general examination of our human test subjects was to be done. Only hours after that I was supposed to feed one group active cholera germs, the other the heat-killed bacteria.

In my doctor's bag were two brown glass bottles, labelled "active" and "inactive", together with a large syringe and a rubber hose for forced feeding, should it become necessary.

As we made our way through the hall of block five, I asked Stark to examine the women, letting him believe I felt an aversion to the female sex. This seemed to amuse him.

A guard opened the door to a cell and I stepped in. The door was shut behind me. All the tiny hairs on my body stood erect. The small window, deep set into the thick and ice-cold stone walls, was far up and blocked with four metal bars. The floor was cold, too. The room sucked up all warmth. I was shivering before I was done placing my utensils on a small wooden table.

A rattling at the door made me turn. The guard opened and the first test subject was shoved in without much ado. I was shocked — the man was naked, his hands cuffed behind his back. The guard remained standing at the door.

My tongue glued itself to my palate. I wanted to shout that there was absolutely no necessity to force all the clothes off that man. But respect and compassion had obviously left this place long ago, and I wondered why seemingly normal people would willingly turn themselves into torture machines.

It gives them power, my mind whispered. I nodded and regretted the gesture at once. The guard narrowed his eyes at me.

I examined the first man, and then the next, and the next. They were all the same: undernourished, maltreated, terrified. They all hoped I would help them, show them mercy, or tell them what was about to happen. As if the truth would have made it easier. I wondered if Stark — who found pleasure in the pain of others — whispered into the women's ears that they are going to die of cholera, strapped to a bunk. And if he was saying it in a way that suggested a sexual favour might earn a woman her freedom. I wouldn't put anything past that man.

The guard led in another man. He looked like those before him, starved and dirty, with ribs only too visible above a sunken abdomen. He was hunched and limping, his feet blackened. Nicholson wouldn't recognise this wreck of a man whom he had once met a long time before.

I placed myself between him and the guard, and slowly lifted my head. My heart was hammering and my face hot as if someone had slapped it repeatedly. He appeared controlled, and kept his eyes fixed on a spot somewhere above my head.

I began the routine auscultation. Like the others, he had a number of bruises and cuts on his torso. I placed my clammy hand on each mark. One had the shape of a shoe. That, and an old scar right next to his spine and the freckles on his shoulders, made my eyes water.

Angry with my weakness, I cleared my throat, squeezed my eyes shut for a moment, and got back to the matter at hand.

I examined his mouth, tongue, and eyes, silently trying to communicate to him that I had a plan, that he could trust me. Although I wasn't too sure what that plan might be.

But he looked determined, as though he had his own

strategy. Without moving his head, his eyes darted towards the guard, then looked back at me. As his lips twitched to the faintest smile, I stopped breathing. A second later, he coughed violently and doubled over, barely able to catch a breath.

I barked at the guard to make haste and take off the cuffs to prevent the man from choking. The confused man stumbled towards Holmes, but stopped halfway, uncertain what would be the safest procedure. I took a step towards him and shot out my hand, ordering him to give me the key.

Holmes was now on the floor, face purple, lips pale. The guard's eyes flew from my outstretched hand to the heap of coughing man. He seemed unable to decide what he should do.

I took another step towards him and kicked him hard in his groin. He caved in with a pitiful huff. I used all my fury to punch his face and kick his side. He hit the floor, but pushed himself up quickly. That was when Holmes's heel made contact with the back of the guard's head.

Any other day, the loud crack would have shocked me. Today, it felt like the greatest relief. We had won our first battle without making too much noise and drawing attention.

'Is he dead?' Holmes asked.

I touched the man's neck and felt a feeble pulse. Blood was dribbling from his nose and pooling on the stone tiles. 'He's alive.' I extracted the key from his fist, told Holmes to turn around, and took off the manacles. Then I took a step back to give him room to take off the guard's clothes and dress himself.

As he pocketed the revolver, he asked casually, 'How long until they expect you to receive another patient?'

'Ten or fifteen minutes at most,' I croaked.

'That should suffice.' Gingerly, he grasped my right hand

and pulled it up to his face. I hadn't noticed that my knuckles were bleeding.

Before he could examine it any further, I whisked my hand away. 'What is your plan?'

'I will break into Nicholson's office and send a telegram to the local police, informing them of a most unfortunate mass breakout. That should make them come with the artillery.' The smug smile put all the usual energy back into his face.

'Listen, Holmes, whatever happens, I must be Anton Kronberg for a little while longer. I'll explain it to you later.'

He nodded, and I said, 'Now, I need to be unconscious. Believably. Knock me out.'

He snorted, looked around, and picked up a small piece of plaster from the floor.

'You want to hit me on the head with that tiny thing?'

'All you need is a little blood,' he said, took a step forward, grabbed my neck, but as with all head wounds it bled profusely.

'Thanks,' I noted wryly and bent down to rub some dirt in my face.

He grinned, and unlocked the door with the guard's latch key.

I watched him leave, then curled up on the floor. My heart was galloping in anticipation and worry, and I wished I could do more than just lie there, pretending to take a nap.

22

L ying on the cold stones, I felt like the eye of a tornado. Holmes was the storm and I was its eye, watching the destruction around me. I shut my eyes again and peered into my own darkness, as I listened to the soft *click click* of blood dripping down onto the floor.

A rap on the door. *The tempest begins.* I remained silent as the knocks became more urgent, then turned into shouts. 'Dr Kronberg? What is going on? I demand you open the door at once!' It was Stark's voice.

Then I heard him fumble the lock to try to force it. Several minutes passed until a spare key was found, and the door was finally opened. Stark stuck his head through the gap, then shouted, 'An escape! Guards! Hurry!' on his way back through the hall.

The blood had drawn a tiny, black pond on the floor, and I let my thoughts tiptoe back to the night at the bog lake.

After a while, Nicholson walked in. I saw him through half-closed eyes. Methodically, he planted one foot on the ground and then the next. A quiet *tap tap.* I pictured him flicking a forked tongue in and out of the slit of his mouth, like a great anaconda tasting the air, trying to detect its next meal.

Then he stuck the tip of his shoe into my abdomen. This, too, he did slowly and deliberately. I had to suppress an angry growl, and the urge to eat him alive. Only a quiet groan escaped my lips and he stopped, put his foot back to the floor, and left me alone.

A great hustle erupted in the hall — people shouting, several gunshots, and Holmes's commanding voice. Two policemen rushed into the cell. One jerked me up to my feet, slapped my face to wake me, while the other cuffed my hands behind my back. I let my head hang low so as not to show the triumphant grin I couldn't quite wipe off my face. They walked me out of the room with a firm grip on the scruff of my neck. The other men were handled the same way — Stark, Nicholson, Bowden, several guards, and the Broadmoor staff. Standing among them was Holmes, looking very pleased with himself. We avoided looking at other.

They loaded us criminals into a cart with two armed officers. The other policemen and Holmes followed in a hansom and Bowden's brougham. It looked as though Holmes had engaged the entire local police force.

On the way to the police station, we passed over a particularly bumpy section of the cobblestone road. I stood up halfway and protested against this inhumane treatment of a medical doctor who had only wanted to save mankind — I did that rather loudly — and then head-butted Nicholson while falling on top of him.

The crack I heard as my forehead made contact with his nose was very satisfactory indeed. The man protested with zest — spitting saliva, blood, and insults at me.

The cart came to a halt, and one of the two policemen slammed me back onto my seat. Nicholson was bleeding copiously, his eyes full of hate, and I was certain that he would have wrung my neck there and then if he could only have freed his hands. My lips twitched to a smile, and I let Nicholson see it. Naturally, it did nothing to improve his mood.

Feeling like a queen on her throne, I rode along. The time of the Club was over.

Not once did I stop to think of consequences. I was a fool.

~

WE ARRIVED at the local police station after a twenty-minute drive.

'Put this man into a separate cell, Inspector. He was the head of the gang, and I must interview him at once,' said Holmes, with the most convincing coldness in his voice. Even the small hairs on the back of my neck believed it, and bristled.

An inspector led me into a small interrogation room and pressed me down onto a stool. He left and locked the heavy iron door. Only a moment later, it was opened. I heard ruffling, the door being locked, and two swift steps taken. Then, Holmes's face appeared in front of mine.

Exceedingly careful, he inspected my head. The cut he had made was irrelevant. The bruise on my forehead did hurt, but it would heal soon enough. He was so focused on examining my superficial wounds with gentle fingers that he didn't notice my gaze.

And, without thinking, I shut my eyes and leant into his touch. He froze, as did I. All that was audible was the rumbling of my heart and the soft hiss of breaths. He moved closer then. For a moment, I believed he would pull me into an embrace. His hands went behind my back; the manacles clicked. and fell to the floor.

'You broke Nicholson's nose.'

'I identified his footprint.' I jerked my chin to Holmes's side where I had seen a boot-shaped bruise.

He straightened up, about to speak, when someone knocked and called, 'The brougham is ready, Mr Holmes.'

'Come,' he said, picking up the manacles. 'I have to put them back on for the time being. I'm to transfer you to London. Yard Headquarters.'

I nodded and crossed my wrists behind my back.

23

I mpatiently, the horses kicked the ground as Holmes walked me over to the carriage and shoved me in. The driver flicked the whip. The brougham made a lurch and smashed my back and cuffed wrists against its wall behind me.

A short moment later, my tingling hands were freed and Holmes took a seat opposite me. 'Officially, I'm on my way to Yard Headquarters to turn you in,' he began. 'Unofficially, Lestrade and I, and twenty other men will take down the other members of the Club. The ones residing at Cambridge will be arrested by the local police there.'

'All right.' I rubbed my red-rimmed wrists. 'But I don't understand your plan of escape. My presence was more or less coincidental. They could have done without me today.'

He waved his hand and snorted. 'There were so many holes in their security system that I must wonder why they chose Broadmoor as a location. After all, several breakouts have been reported there in past years. It's common knowledge that the mortar in the brick walls is soft, and that the bars can easily be dismounted. And even without all those possibilities,' here he threw up his hands, 'the guards, for Christ's sake! They carry revolvers so carelessly, I could have snatched one any time one of those mindless brutes walked by!'

So he hadn't waited for my arrival, or my help. I felt somewhat useless, but it didn't matter. I smiled down at my hands, happy and relieved that all was over. Well, almost... 'What about the man at the Dundee School of Medicine?'

Holmes balled a fist. His knuckles whitened. 'He is as yet unidentified. And it appears that this case is much more complex than we believed. I've wondered for a while now about a possible involvement of the government. You remember that Standrincks is paid through governmental sources?'

I raised my eyebrows.

'Of course you do. So I went to visit my brother—'

'You have a brother?' I interrupted, and he answered with a shrug.

'Mycroft told me—'

'Mycroft? By Jove! Sherlock, Mycroft — what were your parents thinking?'

He stared at me, wide-eyed.

'My apologies. Pray proceed.' I felt rather hot in my face.

After an indignant harrumph, he said, 'My dear brother is working for the government, but likes to believe he *is* the government. Sometimes I do think there is a grain of truth in that. Regardless, Mycroft has no knowledge of any such activities.'

'You believe him?'

'Yes. He is, I fancy, my most trustworthy source when it comes to such things.'

'Any clue on how the Club's research was financed?'

'Ah! But, of course!' said he, his eyes lighting up and energy crackling in his voice. 'What do you think I've been doing these long weeks? Just sitting on my hindquarters, eating porridge, and picking oakum? The Club's supporters included lawyers, bankers, and even men working for the government, though apparently without their superiors' knowledge. Your Superintendent Rowlands helped pay their bills, too. It's a rather long list of names.'

'How many?' I asked cautiously.

'Fifty-four men.'

My hand involuntarily clapped over my mouth, my mind began racing and putting my own small puzzle pieces next to the ones he had provided. The picture grew darker...

Holmes interrupted my thoughts. 'I do believe, however, that the Club reached farther than that. Unfortunately, we have no information whatsoever on the Dundee part. The question remains how far their net extended.'

'But the most important question is *why*,' I answered.

'I thought that was clear from the beginning?'

Slowly, I shook my head. 'I believe the vaccine tests were either pretence, or only part of their goal. I dare say the latter.'

'What goal, precisely?' He leaned forward.

'You asked me how I got Bowden to trust me.'

He nodded. I dropped my gaze to the muddy tips of my boots. Images of the dying woman, and of my hand holding an ether-soaked cloth invaded my mind.

'I had this...mad idea,' I said quietly, 'about using deadly germs for warfare.'

Holmes sat erect like a stick, all tension and awareness.

'Bowden's eyes lit up. But not in surprise. He *knew*.'

'He was already working on it?' Holmes's voice was brisk with shock.

'I cannot tell. But the plan exists, I am absolutely certain.'

We stared at each other and, after a while, I added softly, 'We hacked off one limb, but we didn't kill the monster.'

'No,' he said, throwing his head back against the brougham's wall and shutting his eyes. Then his throat produced a deep growl. 'Someone is at the centre of all this. We will find him in due course.'

I noticed the *we*. Another day, it would perhaps have made me proud. 'I will leave London,' I said.

His eyes opened and he pulled himself up again. After some consideration, he said, 'Yes, that is sensible. It might be the only reasonable thing for you to do. Otherwise, you would be bait.'

I gazed out of the window, feeling empty.

'That is not the reason you leave?' he asked doubtfully.

I shook my head.

'You sent me a letter the day before you fell ill with cholera.'

I nodded.

'You euthanised her?'

I nodded again.

'I would not arrest you for that!' He sounded as if I had said something utterly ridiculous.

'It doesn't matter. Prison or no prison, it doesn't change what I feel. I killed the woman. I should have tried to help her.'

'Hmm.' He narrowed his eyes in consideration. 'If carrying a weakened or even unconscious woman out of a room and past several guards would not have raised suspicion and would not have resulted in her *and* you being killed, then I guess your thinking isn't as illogical as it appears.' His gaze softened. 'I don't believe you could have saved her. Even if you had, they would have found someone else with cholera.'

'Yes,' I replied. 'They would have found another one for *me*. She was delivered to me, and no one else.'

'It is ridiculous to blame yourself!'

'What is it to you anyway?' I snarled.

'So you decide to run away from yourself,' he declared.

'Yes, I do. And from a corrupt medical establishment that abandons an entire sex. I run away from the man at the centre of the Club, from the police, and...' I forced my throat to unfold again, '...and from you.'

His gaze flickered. He looked surprised and, I think, hurt.

I held on to my hands so as not to grab his to comfort him. 'I run away from you because I cannot live next to you, and not understand what it is that draws me to you. And it seems to me that whenever I stoke your emotional side, I hurt you, and that's the last thing I want.'

'You must understand that I have no tendencies to romanticism.' His voice sounded as though he had swallowed glue.

'I know who you are,' I whispered.

Now it was he who stared out of the window. He seemed to argue with himself. After a while, he asked, 'Have you planned your escape?'

'Of course. I will, quite simply, overpower you.' I smirked.

His mouth twitched in response. 'Do you plan to hide in St Giles? I don't believe it's—'

'It's not safe. I know. I have a place far away from London.'

'You do? Where?'

'I won't tell you.'

He waved his hand impatiently. 'You know my abilities!'

'Don't waste your time.' He wouldn't find me. I had bought the cottage using a different name. There was nothing that would link my new home to my old identity.

'That is ridiculous.'

'No, it isn't. As long as the greatest detective cannot find me, no one will.' I didn't mention that if I did tell him where I lived, I would be waiting for him to walk through my front door — every single day. My brain would know he wouldn't, but my heart would disagree.

Silence fell again and, after a long while, I added, 'Promise me that you'll place an advertisement in *The Times*, asking for Caitrin Mae, should your life be in danger or when this case is solved. I'll find you then.'

I noticed his smirk and added, 'I have not used this name before, nor will I ever. I just made it up.'

His eyes turned dark. He produced a nod and turned to observe the countryside. His jaws were working.

Suddenly, with quite a lot of energy that only a good plan could bring, he stated merrily, 'I think it is time for violence.'

'What?'

'It's not *What* — it's *Excuse me!*' He rose from his seat.

I could not place the playful look he had in his eyes.

'Your escape has to appear authentic,' he explained before grabbing both my shoulders, lifting me up, and slamming me against the cab's window. I cried out in surprise.

'My apologies,' he whispered as he lunged to the door, and bolted it. Then he threw himself against it and onto the floor, bellowing like a plumber on too much gin. Finally, my brain clicked and I dropped down next to him, grinning and cursing. We rolled around, kicking and hitting the walls and seats like two kids playing war. The hansom made a lurch as the horses reared and changed their slow gait to a gallop.

'What the devil?' the cabby shouted as he tried to get the animals back under control. Holmes tried to stand up, lost balance and fell onto his back with one arm pinned awkwardly beneath him. I pounced and clamped him down with my knees on either side of his ribcage.

'To hell with the police!' I screamed at the top of my lungs while maintaining a firm grip on his trapped arm. His eyes flared with surprise.

'Give up, Mr Holmes!' I bellowed.

'Never!' he barked, and grabbed a fistful of my waistcoat. One button popped.

'For your own sake!' I screamed, slamming a fist down next to his face. That seemed to cause amusement. He probably thought I had indeed planned to overpower him.

Well, maybe I had.

'You villain shall not escape justice!' he roared, as he shook me by the collar.

'I like you this way,' I said softly, and bent down.

His body went limp, the fist holding my waistcoat offered no resistance, and his pupils widened in shock. I held his gaze as my lips touched the corner of his mouth, asking for permission. He gave me a feeble shove as his eyes lost focus, then his head tilted a little, and his warm breath caressed my face. Eyelids fluttered shut, as softly as a bird's wings. Only then did I kiss him. His lips felt like silk.

All of a sudden, my silly heart left my chest to live in his from that day forward. I wondered whether he noticed the additional weight.

Two metallic clicks pulled my mouth away from his and I spotted the guard's revolver in his hand. Aghast, I sat up. His eyes were aflame as he raised his free arm to fire four shots through the cab's roof.

The horses bolted, the cabby shouted, and we were joggled about like chocolate candy in a box. Soon, the vehicle came to a halt. The driver jumped off and ran away, screaming for help.

Holmes unfolded his protective embrace, shoved me up onto the seat, and rose to his feet in one fluid move.

'Out,' he snarled, yanking the door open.

I did as he asked and climbed onto the driver's seat, leaving him alone inside the carriage. I knew that my feelings for him would never be returned. And I wasn't sure why I felt that way for him. Was it because the two of us had gone through an ordeal together? Was it because his mind and mine seemed to know one another? Shouldn't this be a matter of the heart, and not the mind? I had no answer. I felt lost, confused, and utterly inappropriate.

Could a woman love two men? I shook my head, and gave the horses a good flick. I needed wind in my face.

After we had gone from of the cabby's view, Holmes climbed up and sat down next to me.

'Where did you learn to drive a horse carriage?' he demanded gruffly.

'I grew up with... Never mind. It's not complicated, really,' I answered with a thin voice, not at all eager to engage in distractive small talk, or any kind of conversation for that matter.

'That was far from appropriate for a woman of your social standing.'

'Begging your pardon? You are the last person I would expect to care for social standards. Besides, I never pretended to be a woman of the higher classes, and you seem to ignore the fact that, as a woman who looks like a man, I have no social standing whatsoever. By kissing you, all I have rattled is your composure. But you already seem to be getting yourself back together without much effort. In but a moment you'll be your old self.'

'Needless to say,' he muttered to himself.

'If you wanted an ordinary woman, you'd be married, and father to a gaggle of annoying children,' I replied acidly.

It was a useless conversation, and we both knew it. Unspeaking, we drove the long way to London. I steered the cab into Tottenham Court Road, and stopped. My anger had evaporated to leave a hole of shame in my chest.

'I apologise,' I said softly.

He took up the reins, nodded once, and said, 'It was nothing.'

'I know.'

I climbed off the brougham. The moment my feet touched the cobblestones, he flicked the whip and drove away. Not once did he look back.

END

Keep reading for a preview of book 3

THE FALL

Preview of Anna Kronberg Book 3

Two Men

And soon the rotting corpses tainted the air and poisoned the water supply, and the stench was so overwhelming that hardly one in several thousand was in a position to flee the remains of the Tartar army.

Gabrielle De' Mussi, 1348, on the Siege of Caffa

For this moment, this one moment, we are together. I press you to me. Come, pain, feed on me. Bury your fangs in my flesh. Tear me asunder. I sob, I sob.

Virginia Woolf

Wednesday Night, October 22nd, 1890

Cold metal pressed my head hard against the mattress. Two sharp clicks and the scent of gun oil sent my heart jumping out my throat. The muzzle was flush against my temple. If fired, the bullet would rip straight through my brain, driving blood and nerve tissue through the mattress and down onto the floor. And if the gun should be tilted just a little, the bullet would circle inside my skull, leaving a furrow in the bone and pulp in its wake.

I don't know why those were my first thoughts. What does one normally think when faced with imminent death?

'Get up,' a male voice cut through the dark. 'Slowly.'

I opened my eyes.

'Sit over there,' he rasped, waving a bullseye lantern towards the table. I rose and shuffled over to a chair. My knees felt like water. I sat, and the backrest squeaked in protest.

A match was struck, illuminating a face chiselled in hard-wood, and cracked by tension and age. Sulphur hung in the air. A man of approximately fifty years sat across from me. He held the match to a candle, and cast the room into unsteady light.

He sat back and stared at me. Waves of goose bumps rolled over my skin. He seemed to be waiting for me to speak, to ask him what he was doing there, and why he was holding me at gunpoint. But I had no words.

'You are good at hiding,' he said.

Not good enough, though. I swallowed. Would I beg at some point? Should I even? Probably not. It would be more likely that a word — a wrong word — would end my life in an instant.

Suddenly, my ears picked up a sound. Nearly inaudible. I tried to analyse it, play it back in my head to understand what had caused it, what it meant. It wasn't one of the noises an old house makes when the wind leans into it.

The man interrupted my thoughts. 'Last spring, a group of physicians were captured by the police and led to trial. Only two months later, they found their end at the gallows.'

I remembered that day. I'd sat on this very same chair and read about the hanging of sixteen medical men, along with the superintendent of Broadmoor Lunatic Asylum and four of his guards. All convicted for murder and manslaughter. And I still remembered the fear that had crept in when I realised that not one of the articles reported on the experiments the men had performed on abducted paupers. That same fear now raised its head — and I knew what the noise behind me meant: the floorboards had produced a lone pop. The tiny hairs on my neck rose in response. As though to assess the danger lurking there.

'All but one,' the man interrupted.

My neck began to ache. There was another noise, behind me and very close: the soft hiss of air through nostrils.

Shock widened my senses with a snap. Was the man behind me a backup? Someone to break my neck, if needed? I coughed, flicked my gaze toward the window and back again. For a short moment I shut my eyes to examine the reflection burned into my mind: the small prick of candlelight, the table, the man sitting, myself in a nightgown, and a tall, slender figure behind me. I opened my eyes, hoping the behaviour of the man facing me would tell me more about the other.

'Only Dr Anton Kronberg made his escape. He even overpowered Mr Sherlock Holmes. Odd, isn't it.'

My fingertips grew ice cold. The Club! Holmes had given this dubious title to the group of physicians that had been testing deadly bacteria on workhouse inmates. It had taken us months to round them up. Yet we had been unable to identify the head of the organisation that had caused so much suffering and death. Ever since my escape to the Downs, I'd been afraid he would find me and take revenge. I eyed the man in front of me, wondering why he was talking to me at all, and what he planned to do to me before pulling the trigger.

'Imagine my surprise when I finally found Anton Kronberg. He lives in a small village in Germany. Scrapes by as a carpenter.' A smile tugged at the man's face.

I couldn't breathe.

'The man has a single child. A daughter. But you know that, of course.' Again that half smile. 'Tell me, *Doctor* Anna Kronberg, what shall I do with you now?'

'What have you done to my father?'

He flashed a row of yellowed teeth. I made an effort to slow my frantic heart, and stop my imagination from showing me the corpse of my father. I forced my senses outward, to the man behind me. He seemed calm. No hitch in his breathing, no quickening. All was going according to plan, it appeared.

'You do say rather little,' the man in front of me said.

'You have not asked a single question,' I croaked.

No audible reaction from the man behind. The man facing me smiled a thin line and fingered his gun. His eyes were glued to my face, as mine flicked between his and the weapon's hammer. He repeatedly pulled and released it. *Click-click. Click-click.*

'Will you admit to these accusations?' *Click-click.*

'Your accusations must have escaped my notice.'

The clicking stopped. His eyes flicked sideways and back at me again, as though he wanted to check with the other man, but could not reveal that man's presence by looking at him directly. Behind me, I heard a faint smack. It made me think of wet lips being pulled apart. Was he smiling? For a heartbeat I had the insane thought it was Holmes.

'Do I amuse you?' asked the man in front of me. *Click-click. Click-click.* He had both elbows leisurely propped on his thighs, his weapon held loosely in his right hand. The lantern at his feet seemed to illuminate only the triangle of knees, hands, and gun. The light reflecting off the hammer's silvery tip — polished by repeated toying — stung my eyes.

'I find you remarkable unfunny,' I answered.

He waited. We both did. And then I made a mistake. 'What does a man from the military want from me?' It was only a guess based on the few things I had seen: how he moved, how he expected instant obedience, how he held the revolver, his physique.

'What do you know?' he snapped, just before noticing that he, too, had made a mistake.

'You broke into my cottage to press a gun to my head and tell me things I already know. There is a man behind me who is very calm, approximately six feet tall, and rather lean. I'm guessing that he is the brain of this operation, while you are merely the brute.'

There was no time to flinch before his fist hit my temple.

WHISPERS TICKLED MY CONSCIOUSNESS. I heard a groan; it came from inside my chest. My head thrummed, and blue flashes of light flickered across the inside of my eyelids. I found myself on my mattress, my hands bound across my stomach. I inhaled a slow breath, and the whispering stopped. Blinking, I turned my head. Two men sat at the table, and looked to me as though expecting to be served tea and biscuits, plus the latest gossip.

'Funny,' I said.

The taller of the two pulled up his eyebrows. 'You do realise that having seen my face, your chances of survival are diminished?'

I said nothing.

'Shall we continue, then? How did you escape? And how the deuce did *you* overpower Mr Holmes?'

Oh. Well. How indeed could a woman of my statue knock out a man who was said to never have lost a fist fight? I almost laughed. My throat tightened as I thought back to the day Holmes and I went separate ways. I certainly wasn't about to explain the details to these two men. Or to anyone, for that matter. I cleared my sticky throat and said, 'It was rather simple. I kissed him.'

The tall man's nostrils flared. He threw back his head and barked a laugh. A heartbeat later, he recovered from the emotional outbreak. Turning to the other man he said, 'Colonel, what about a drop of tea?'

At once, the Colonel stood and made for my kitchen. I heard a match being struck, the soft hiss of the oil lamp followed by the clonking of earthenware. The hearth was still hot. I used it to get a little warmth into the cottage on chilly autumn nights. In winter, I would have used the fireplace, too. But it seemed that there wouldn't be a winter for me here.

More wood was thrown onto the embers. The tall man observed me silently, and I realised he had come to decide whether I should be shot immediately, or maybe a little later.

While we waited for the tea, he said, 'We've learnt a few things about you, Dr Kronberg. But there are gaps I'd like filled.' He approached, bent over me, grabbed my neck, and pulled me up into a sitting position. Casually, he sat on the mattress next to me. 'You lived in London disguised as a male medical doctor for four years. You must have met Mr Holmes over the course of the summer or the autumn of 1889, is that correct?'

I nodded, knowing my trembling chin betrayed my shock.

'A little more information would help extend your lifespan.'

I felt the blood drain from my face and drop to my toes. 'I met Mr Holmes at Hampton Water Treatment Works in the summer of last year. A cholera victim had been found floating in the water and Scotland Yard wanted us to provide expert opinions. Mr Holmes saw through my disguise, but decided not to report me to the police. The corpse bore signs of abduction and maltreatment, but the evidence was weak and the Yard did not think it worth investigating.'

I looked up at him. He was waiting for me to continue. And so I did, weaving lies and facts into one, 'There was very little to go on, and Mr Holmes soon lost interest in the case. Or so I believed. Meanwhile, I did research on tetanus at Guy's and later visited Robert Koch's laboratory in Berlin. I was able to obtain tetanus germs in pure culture; it was a sensation, and the papers reported it widely. You are aware of this, of course.'

He dipped his head a fraction, and I continued. 'Only a few days later, Dr Gregory Stark invited me to give a presentation at Cambridge Medical School and I came into contact with all the members of what Mr Holmes later called the *Club*.'

'How charming.'

'I knew it couldn't have been Bowden,' I said. 'You, it turns out, were the man at the centre.' Holmes and I believed at first that Dr Bowden was the head of the Club. Doubts about the importance of his role surfaced only at the very end of our investigation. But we could prove nothing, and we had no clues to who the leader might've been.

'I am merely a bystander,' the man said with a wink.

My skin crawled. 'The bystander pulling the strings?'

He said nothing for a long moment. Just looked at me as though not quite sure what to ask next. I jumped when he leant closer. He pulled a blanket over my shoulders and smiled. It made me think of how I killed my hens: I calmed them, caressed their heads and backs until they were entirely unsuspecting. And then I cut their heads off.

'You infiltrated the Club and brought them down with the help of Mr Holmes,' he said.

I forced my eyes to look into his and remain steady. 'Not quite, although in hindsight, even I could possibly interpret it as such.'

He leant back a little, cocked his head, and nodded at me to continue.

And so I did. 'Just after I returned from Berlin I was mugged and badly injured. I needed a surgeon, but whom to ask? Certainly not my colleagues. So I told a friend to find Dr Watson, who — like Holmes — knew my secret. That is how I met Holmes again, and only two days later he told me about his suspicions — that someone was conducting medical experiments on paupers in Broadmoor Lunatic Asylum. I thought he was out of his mind.'

The man turned to his companion, and I got the impression that he grew impatient. My time was running out.

'I started working at London Medical School, developing vaccines against tetanus. We also had the prospect of a cholera vaccine. But we knew that wouldn't come without sacrifices.' Images of a dying woman invaded my mind. I shoved them away. 'Holmes kept insisting that what I was doing was wrong, and that I should instead be helping him build a case against my colleagues.'

'Mr Holmes would never have asked you for your assistance. You are a liar, my dear,' he declared.

For once a reaction I had anticipated. 'You are correct. He would have never asked such a thing from just anyone.' I paused. It sickened me what I had to say next. 'But Holmes and I are made of the same material. He was fascinated by a woman as intelligent as he and equally strong-willed. And I fell for him because I had never met such an observant and sharp man in my life. That is the reason I saved his life in Broadmoor and the reason he set me free.' And I remembered the kiss, that singular kiss, and turned my gaze away to look out of the small window where night slowly retreated and the sky paled to greet the new day. Would I see the sun? Maybe it did not matter much. I had seen it many times already.

I gazed back at the man and said, 'I know you want something from me, or you would not have given me the time to utter a single word. If you allow me to make a guess — you need a bacteriologist to continue your work. I am your first choice, but you do not trust me. Naturally.'

He smiled again. It was worse than a gun pressed to my head. 'No, I do not trust you in the least. And yes, I require the services of a bacteriologist. Although you are the best to be found in England, you are also the one who carries the greatest risk. I need to be certain I have your loyalty.'

What could I possibly offer? My life? He already had it in his hands.

'Of course, you could choose to be shot right away. But decide quickly now, or I will do it for you.'

I gazed down at my hands, anticipating the moment I would drive a blade into the man's throat. Slowly, I let go of all the air in my lungs. 'Am I to isolate pathogens for warfare?'

Another warm smile.

'You remind me of him,' I whispered. His stunned expression opened a wide spectrum of possibilities for me. He blinked the shock away so quickly, that I wasn't sure I had even seen it.

'You have my loyalty,' I answered.

All I got as a response was a scant nod. 'Drink your tea,' he said, and filled my cup.

Finally I noticed the peculiar situation — the brute had made tea, the brain served it. I gazed at the two men. 'What did you put in it?'

'Chloral,' the taller answered lightly.

'Ah,' I exhaled. 'How much?'

'A few drops.'

I nodded and took the cup. The harmless-looking tea produced circular ripples just before I tipped it into my mouth. The brew carried a peculiar sting. 'You never introduced yourself,' I noted.

'My apologies. This is my friend and trustworthy companion Colonel Sebastian Moran, and I am Professor James Moriarty.'

Slowly, my surroundings unhinged. I looked at the window which seemed unnaturally far off. Had it not been rectangular a few minutes ago?

'I forgot to mention a small detail,' said Professor Moriarty, his voice reverberating in my skull, words melting into one another. 'By the time you regain consciousness, your father will be my hostage. Should you do anything that could jeopardise our work or my safety, he will die immediately and, I must say, rather painfully.'

The world tipped and the table approached with shocking speed.

The Fall is available at all major retailers.

www.silent-witnesses.com
www.anneliewendeberg.com

Acknowledgments

I am so grateful for my husband's deep love and his belief in my writing (besides other obsessions). He and our friend Martha Schattenhofer had to endure the awful first drafts and luckily slapped them over my head rather often. I survived, as you may have noticed.

Many thanks go to Ronald Kötteritzsch, who loved even the early versions of *The Devil's Grin*.

I am deeply indebted to my faithful reviewers at www.thenextbigwriter.com. Especially T.M. Hobbs, who let me torture her all the way through, and Phyl Manning, who took me aside and told me to stop babbling and start **showing** things.

J.E. Nissley and Nancy DeMarco, two of the most talented writers I have ever had the pleasure to come across and the honour to review their work and be reviewed by them. The humbling number of authors at TNBW giving me advice and helping me to become a better writer (uh, I did say **writer**, now, didn't I?) shall be given names here: Q.X.T. Rhazmeulen, Bonnie Milani, dagnee, David Reynolds, C.E.

Jones, Debbie Lampi, and John DeBoehr. And special thanks to Janet Taylor-Perry for yet another round of typo-detection.

Another brilliant author, who offered invaluable help, and whose advice and mere interest in my writing still makes me giddy, is Paul Negri.

I'm quite relieved that this thing survived the scrutinizing eyes of Alistair Duncan from the Sherlock Holmes Society London. Phew!

The last was the first: Ruben Zorilla, who accidentally received a full-length draft and fell in love with the story. Thank you, Ruben, for your praise and support. You were my first ever reader!

I'd like to thank the great people at the Asexuality Visibility Network (www.asexuality.org) for sharing their views of and experiences with asexuality – one potential facet of Sherlock Holmes – with me. And a big thank you goes to David Jay, for letting me bug him with so many (awkwardly private) questions about the many shades of asexuality.

To all of you, I do the full prostration (picture me touching my knees with my nose).

∾

Many thanks to the Kronberg Street Team for beta reading this new and revised edition: Susan Meikle, Lou Valentine, Rich Lovin, David Harrison, and Josef Zens.

And to all the lovely and crazy people who read the stuff I write, and who have accompanied me on my wild ride: This journey would have been so fucking boring without you!

Oops! I said the f-word. AGAIN!

And to Tom Welch, friend, proofreader, and comrade in arms: Thank you for everything! Especially the thing with the loom :)

Made in the USA
San Bernardino, CA
23 November 2017